KU-437-124

THE OPAL SEEKERS

THE OPAL SEEKERS

by

RAY HARRIS

THE CHILDREN'S PRESS
LONDON AND GLASGOW

PRINTED AND MADE IN GREAT BRITAIN

CONTENTS

CHAPTER ONE

THE LAUGH

"HOW DID I sleep? Don't be funny *all* the time! . . . Sleep!"

The big man snarled the words at George Warburton, leaning forward through the doorway of a travel-grimed tent as he spoke. Then, trouser cuffs caught up in slovenly fashion on unlaced boots, he stepped right out and straightened, one hand on the projecting ridge pole.

"Sleep!" he said again, angrily. "With those cursed dingoes howling for hours, ringing the camp all night! What I want to know is, why the heck did you have to come out into dingo country?"

"Aw, snap out of it, Don," his companion said quietly. He was an older man, powerfully built and as tall as the other, but in the brilliant morning sun, his face looked sallow and haggard. "I can't help it if you hate dingoes the way you do. We're after opals, aren't we? And this is the country they're in, wild dogs or no wild dogs."

"Sure," the other sneered again. "This is the country for opals, ain't it? That must be why we've found a dozen third-grade stones in three months. . . . Three months! Not enough to pay for the tucker we brought." His voice rose to a shout. "And you call yourself a prospector, Warburton! Why . . ."

He stopped. Warburton had said nothing and made no movement but there was a glint in his eyes that made Don Graster suddenly afraid. In the silence that followed, his ugly scowl was replaced by a look half uneasy, half cunning. Again George Warburton spoke quietly:

"Yes, I'm a prospector, Don, and a good one and you know it. But there's a deuce of a lot of luck in prospecting whether it's for gold or opals or anything else, and you know that too, or you should. We haven't had the breaks that's all. But I reckon we'll have a good look round across to the south there to-day. If we find better prospects we'll shift camp to-morrow. Here, have a drink of tea and some breakfast. You'll feel a whole lot better."

Graster took the fire-blackened can by one side of its handle and forced a grin.

"Okay, okay. Sorry, George. It's these darned dingoes ringing us round all night that are getting me down." He paused, still holding the can. "As a matter of fact I thought . . . well, if y' didn't mind, I'd lay off to-day and . . . well, and catch up on a bit o' sleep."

Warburton, about to answer, stopped and frowned. A sharp pain had cut across his forehead. He knew what that meant. An attack of malaria working up. . . . Rotten luck. Well, he'd take a crack of quinine and keep going while he could, anyway. Still frowning, he reached into his trouser pocket and drew out his pipe.

"Okay, then," he said to Graster. "Lay off for the day if that's how it is. In that case I'll just take old Blaze and a canteen and get away."

Within half an hour, astride his big, brown, game-headed gelding he rode away southward. He travelled light, as he said he would, some food in the saddle bag beside the canteen, a hammer-headed pick hung from the other side of the saddle as well as his rifle, muzzle down, in its saddle-bucket in front. The big horse stepped out freely, for he could walk five miles an hour, as fast as many horses can jog. Warburton looked back once to see Graster standing leaning on the tent pole, but he was too far off to see the tigerish snarl on his partner's face. Then he turned and rode steadily into the mirage.

His search for opal signs throughout the fiery day proved a vain one, and he rode back to camp at sunset.

But he rode back to a circle of dead ashes and a criss-cross of naked tent poles!

The prospector had no illusions concerning his plight . . . Graster had gone north, taking the three remaining horses, the tent, all the food and all the water; and the little bag of opals. But even that wasn't the worst. Standing, bridle rein on arm at his horse's shoulder, Warburton's mouth set grimly. Graster would have both water and food to spare, yet he had taken the lot. But that was only part of his cunning. He would have seen the plain signs of malaria in the older man's sallow face. And he had taken all the quinine! . . . He meant the sick man to die; if not of thirst then of fever; to die alone in the wilderness.

Warburton glanced at the setting sun, then at the stripped camp about him. Eastward to the cattle stations was his only chance, he knew; if it *was* a chance; if his thirsty horse could make the crossing of the wide-flung limestone ridges that barred the way to the stations. . . . Graster knew about those terrible ridges, too. . . . The swine!

Warburton decided to rest his horse for six hours. He hobbled him out on a nearby patch of desert herbage and, thirsty though he was, the big, hardy gelding began cropping the dry fodder. Back at the camp, the man settled himself into his upturned saddle and tried to sleep, but his pains were ominously worse. They meant fever to-morrow or the day after at latest.

He started three hours before dawn and, by sunrise, had covered over twenty miles. Then came the heat and the mirages, heat that seemed to sear his aching temples; yet he rode on and on, hour after hour. And at noon he came to the edge of the limestone. He dismounted, unsaddled and hobbled his horse and lay down, his head in the saddle's small shadow.

An hour later he re-saddled, swallowed a half dozen mouthfuls of the half pint of hot water left in the canteen and rode into the ridges.

They were ridges of bare, reddish limestone, tumbled and twisted in strange rings, as if the slime of an ocean bed had surged up, boiling, into the sunlight and suddenly turned to stone. They flung up a reddish glare that hurt his eyes and their strange, marble smoothness strewn, though sparsely, with water-worn conglomerate, made dangerous footing, even for a horse unshod, as Warburton's was. The sick man spoke, his words half gasped above the resolute clip-clop of the horse's hoofs:

"Watch it, Blaze, old timer. . . . Break a leg . . . dead easy!"

The big gelding seemed well aware of the danger and picked his way with care, never making a false step. But he had had no water for 30 hours now, and clearly the treacherous going was tiring him fast. By mid-afternoon he was plodding wearily. And then, as though in pity for man and horse who travelled undaunted into that nightmare world, a wide, grey cloud crept up into the northern sky till it blanketed the savage sun. And it spread westward and blackened as the long day waned.

It was nearing sunset now. The prospector's aching eyes scanned the eastern horizon, but they could find no end to the terrible ridges.

The almost beaten gelding plodded over a ridge, across a narrow valley and up on to the crest of one more ridge, his sick rider reeling in the saddle. By then the sun had set and the light was failing. In the north the cloud had turned blue-black and lightning flickered across it. And then, as though a lamp had been blown out, darkness was suddenly around them.

Warburton reined in. He could guess what the darkness meant . . . that the thickened cloud had reached far enough westward to blot out the very last of the twilight, and that, out of the darkness, a storm was racing upon him, a storm that would kill him. For the first time, with the sickness he had fought all day pulsing at his temples, despair sprang into his eyes. There had been no rain in the inland for two years; yet now, and within minutes, a storm rain would be lashing this desolation, lashing round his horse and him. For there was no tree nor shrub in the darkness about him, nor even a boulder he could lie against. The wind-driven rain would chill his fever-racked body to the bone. Raving, racked with shivering, he would die here in the darkness.

The lightning stabbed the black sky now. By the blue light of its flashes, his prospector's eyes searched the ridge surface. A strange rock surface, smooth marbly limestone strewn with water-worn conglomerate; limestone far too hard to show a hoofmark.

And then a savage fork of lightning split the northern sky, arched overhead and flooded the ridge with a livid blue light; and Warburton saw a strange thing. Fifty yards ahead, five shining lines converged on a point like the giant spokes of a great, broken wheel! Five lines, each perhaps four inches thick, that reached across the surface of stone. Next instant the flash was gone and the lines vanished with it.

But the man had seen the spot they converged upon. He dismounted heavily and led his horse towards it. When he reached it he saw in the next flash a small cavity or tunnel, perhaps two feet in diameter, roofed over with the same level limestone that was all around. The tunnel drove obliquely into the ridge side but sloped steeply downwards. He bent over it quickly and peered into its blackness. At the same time a faint odour assailed him. He straightened and grunted. He knew that smell . . . Dingoes! So that was it! This was a dingo lair and those shining lines caught by the lightning flash were just their pads, the stone surface of the ridge polished by the feet of the dogs converging on the den from their hunting. That meant there must be water within a few miles at most. It must have taken years for those five pads to form like that and probably only in a certain light and from a certain angle would you even see them. And, as for this hole, set flush with the rock surface, unless you walked or rode right on to it you would never see it. And how many men came here? If the myalls knew of it they'd keep it to themselves. Cattle-men, would look at the bare ridges and ride on. Prospectors would glance at the limestone and ride on also. For limestone is one of the least promising of all surface indications. But, here was shelter. He would drive out the dogs and steal their den!

The gelding stood still behind him, his big game head hanging low at last. Swiftly, yet with hands that shook, Warburton stripped the saddle and bridle and half-hobbled him. He patted the horse's drooping neck. "You'll get a big drink darned soon now, old timer," he said, then he stopped, picked up four stones, dropped to his hands and knees and deliberately crawled into the tunnel. The smell of the dogs was at once about him but his body blocked out the lightning flashes and he could see nothing at all. The rock under his hands and knees was jagged, as if it were the bottom of a crevice. Next moment, grasping a stone in his right hand, he threw it hard into the end of the tunnel and, as he threw, he shouted.

He half expected the dogs would rush past him

and away. Instead, his voice flung out like a sudden cry in a great, empty theatre, lost, strangely remote from him, yet strangely amplified till he scarcely recognised it as his own. But hard upon the one shout came echoes, first one, then another, then a dozen together! Multiple echoes that a theatre, no matter how vast, cannot produce. Then the truth dawned on him. The dingo tunnel led into a cavern; a cavern that was very big, its roof arching high above an underground abyss.

There are those who say Fate jeers at a man's despair; or flings him hope and laughs as he struggles to snatch at riches. George Warburton lay, next morning, on a wide rock ledge beside a tiny fire of dry mulga sticks brought yesterday tied in a bundle to his saddle. He watched the firelight reach out and lose itself in pitch darkness, then glanced up to where it struck the low rock roof leaning out over the ledge; not the roof of the cave, for that was high above a chasm that seemed bottomless, but a kind of sloping false roof jutting over the wide ledge.

Outside the cave the rain that had swept the ridge last night had filled little shallow basins in the floor of the little valley at the ridge foot. The prospector had gone out after the storm had passed and watched his thirsty horse still drinking from one of them, and had filled the canteen from another. He lay now in the shelter that had saved his life; lay still, warm and dry. Even the rock he lay on was warm, warm as the air about him, and not from the tiny fire. His fever, that had risen to muttering delirium last night, was less again now. He looked up again at the sloping roof above the ledge. The rock outside was limestone. But this ledge was sandstone; its roof, also was sandstone.

Suddenly he was sitting up. His eyes, long accustomed to reading the meaning of rocks, knew this stone roof for a certain kind of sandstone. It was the queer, soft gritstone beloved of opal seekers. Sometimes, clinging under such rock as this . . .

He got to his feet, moved ten feet along the ledge and farther back under the rock canopy. Then he was reaching a trembling hand to what he saw.

Even as he did, and all in an instant, the vast cave was full of a terrible sound that seemed to spring upon him out of the silence; a deafening laugh, cackling and horrible, that rose and swelled in peal after mad peal and again, peal after peal, as though Fate or devils had waited to see his shaking hand reach out. As suddenly as it began it ceased; but jumbled echoes flung back and round, swelling as the laugh had done, shouting from near and beyond and above and below in the darkness. The man listened, petrified, and beads of sweat sprang into the tense furrows of his drawn face. His rifle was back near the fire where he had laid it on the rock. As he moved towards it his eyes searched the blackness beyond the brief firelight but there was nothing —right or left or before him, nothing. Still he stared into the darkness, stared while the echoes died one by one till at last there was silence, save for the faint flutter of the fire and his own fevered breathing.

He waited a moment longer, then reached into his pack, whirled about and scrambled back under the arch of the gritstone roof, the light pick in hand. He swung the pick with swift, skilled strokes, gouging at what clung to the arching gritstone. As he gouged and sweated, he jerked small stones from the lumps, rough stone that had shown black in a match flame, black with bright red bars around them. Scarcely pausing, he set them beside him on the rock floor. Minutes passed but he did not notice. And with the minutes the pile of black stones grew. He paused at last, his panting hoarse in his ears; hoarse and strangely hollow. But, as though awaiting his pause, the terrible laugh came again, pealing out as before, jeering and menacing, echoed and amplified, till it seemed to the man's sick brain that he was surrounded in a world of devils, hearing their shrieks as in a nightmare. "You have found a fortune! And now we have you!"

With fumbling fingers he thrust the black stones into his shirt against his skin, stumbled along the ledge and caught up his saddle and canteen, stumbled on and out into the sun-drenched world above.

Behind him in the echoing darkness a saddle bag lay where he had tossed it and the rifle barrel glinted red in the glow of the dying fire.

CHAPTER TWO

THE RESCUE

AT THE road junction young Geoff Mason swung the farm truck carefully into the long bitumen road, wet from a quick storm shower, that led away west towards the town. The road was straight and he had seen, as he made the turn, that there was no vehicle in sight, either up the road or down. There wouldn't be, he decided, just at midday like this, and a hot time of year for tourists.

Geoff was only sixteen and so slightly built that he looked younger but he had a special "farm licence" for driving and had qualified for a full licence because he had proved himself a really good driver.

The truck began to feel the long slope ahead now, and the speedo dropped back to twenty. It hung there however, and when, near the top, the slope eased, the engine began to pick up again. A moment more and Geoff could see down the farther side. His glance left the empty road, already drying in patches, to take in the unkempt paddocks on either side. And suddenly his foot whipped from the accelerator to the brake pedal. The heavy truck swayed a little under the drag of her brakes but she held the road. Then she was grinding to a stop.

Geoff's hand was out to cut the switch, but on the instant he changed his mind, slammed the gears into low and swung the wheel. The truck heeled over as she nosed down into the wide ditch beside the road.

A good forty yards from the road and perhaps thirty from the netting fence fringing the ditch, a long, sleek sports car lay completely upside down, its wheels in the air, the front ones still spinning slowly. It lay on a steep slope that broke off abruptly on the very edge of a deep twenty-foot cutting, a cutting apparently made by road workers. The slope was so steep that Geoff marvelled that the car did not slide and crash over the cutting's edge. Obviously she had skidded on that most treacherous of surfaces, a dry bitumen road suddenly sluiced with a heavy shower. She had swung broadside, dived into the ditch, then simply plunged straight through the netting fence. She had carried a panel away completely but it was that that had actually stopped her, stopped her from hurtling into the great cutting. Instead, she had swung again and rolled over, crushing and tearing aside her low-built hood and tearing away her rakish windscreen supports. The top of her right-hand door was within a foot of what was virtually a twenty-foot cliff.

And thrust out from under the door line was a man's head. Its eyes protruded. One cheek and tensed forehead showed purplish black above a grey moustache. The other cheek was pressed cruelly into the sparsely grassed gravel on the slope: And the man's eyes looking at Geoff held an agonised appeal. Geoff took in all that as his truck lurched across the ditch. He sent it smashing through the torn fence panel, then swung right. His quick glance searched the ground for a pole or tree that would serve for a lever. All he saw was a few half-rotted limbs that he knew would be no use at all. Without stopping the truck he straightened her out till he had room to back up, then reversed and worked her back till the tray was close to the overturned car. Leaving the engine running, he yanked up the seat, jerked out a stout rope and ran round behind the smashed car.

It was only then that the precarious position of the car was evident to him. One slight jerk and it would slide the inches necessary to send it crashing twenty feet into the cutting bottom. But to tie the rope to anyone of the upturned wheels and pull from it, would most surely drag the big car and kill the man pinned under that door top. He looked over on to the cutting, nodded grimly, and at once began paying the rope down into it. That done, he ran down the long side of the cutting till he could drop into the bottom, then back along its floor till he could see the car's upturned wheels leaning out over him. Then he tied the dangling rope loosely round his waist and began to climb.

Six feet from the top he looked up and the car above him seemed on the very point of sliding. With foot and hand he drew himself closer. The door handle three inches from that bloated face . . . he must tie the rope to that. The wide door seemed to cant towards him, the whole car seemed somehow to balance on that door edge. From beneath the door the man's head protruded but Geoff could see only one cheek and the back of it now, a mat of grizzled hair pushed awry.

Next moment the youngster was braced against the cutting face and reaching with both hands to the door handle. The rope fitted in snugly round the massive shank of the handle. He tied his knot slowly. One smallest jerk and a ton and a half of metal would be upon him.

But the knot was tied. Slowly he let the weight of the rope end from his hand and the rope was hanging from the door handle. He could see the man trying to move his head. Then he himself was swinging down quickly from hold to hold, then running along the bottom once more and back up the slope.

Three minutes later he was looking out of the truck cab to see the car upturned no longer but on its side, held there by the rope taut from its door handle to the truck's table. With a quick movement he locked down the handbrake of the truck then ran back.

He rounded the car just in time to see a very fat man sitting up. But he was not alone, for in his lap sat a lady as large as himself. The man had one arm round her. His other hand held to his neck. And the bloated face was moving. The mouth was wide open and the man was taking in vast gulps of air. After each gulp he exhaled with a noise like steam escaping from a Westinghouse brake. It seemed he would never have enough air. As he gulped his eyes protruded, then, between gulps, his tongue. Suddenly he spoke, but his voice was no more than a half whisper. He addressed, not Geoff, but the lady on his lap.

"*Marie, ma chère!*" he cried, removing his hand from his own neck and touching her cheek tenderly.

By way of answer the lady raised her head from his shoulder. Geoff saw her eyes open, then grow wide with wonder.

"*Mon Henri! Mon cher Henri!*" she cried. She flung her arms about him and Monsieur Henri's arms went round her—that is, they went as far as possible. They were short arms and Madame was of a circumference very considerable. Next moment both Monsieur and Madame were talking at top speed.

Geoff was vastly relieved as he watched them and listened. He saw they were the only people in the car; and instead of limp corpses they were very much alive. As Madame talked, her hands fluttered to Monsieur's purple face and then to his neck. A ring flashed on one of the soft white hands. Geoff knew little of diamonds, but when the hand was still he wondered if he had ever seen a ring like that one. But while her hands fluttered Madame's tongue poured forth a word torrent the like of which Geoff certainly had never heard! And suddenly he wanted to laugh. He had acquired a little French at school but of the torrents that poured from Madame and Monsieur he understood not a single word.

But next moment Monsieur looked up and saw him. He pointed and Madame also looked. Then she was on her feet with a speed he could not have thought possible to her; and no sooner was his lap clear of his loved one than Monsieur also was afoot. His next move, however, took Geoff completely by surprise. There was a shriek like that of a lost soul and two fat arms were round him and he was being kissed violently on both cheeks. That done, his assailant held him firmly while Madame kissed him; then Monsieur's hand was back again to his neck.

"Look, Marie," he cried. "*Ce jeune homme*, ee 'ave save ze neck!—Oooh,—ze neck!" The fat man blew out his cheeks, then thrust forward his head as though to make sure it would not fall off after all. He groaned as he did so, the deepest groan Geoff had ever heard.

"Ze—what you call 'im?—ze breathe I cannot do, *non*! Ze neck 'e is *guillotiné* and 'e cannot take ze air! Oooooooooooh!"

The agony in the last long-drawn word was too much for the lady. She flew to the speaker, her hands once more fluttering at his bruised neck. Geoff himself took a long breath but less in sympathy with the victim than in relief that he was clear of those vehement embraces. He listened to the renewed word torrent and grinned to think of the scores of French verbs he had absorbed at school, to find now that he could understand these people only when they spoke broken English. Still, it seemed to him that no one but a Frenchman could make anything of this high-speed talk. He glanced back at the road and wondered that no car had yet topped the hill. Then he realised that it was scarcely more than ten minutes ago that he had come over the crest himself and seen Monsieur's wrecked car. He turned back and put a hand on the old Frenchman's shoulder.

"Just stand clear, will you, sir?" he said. "That car's not safe like that for too long. I'll give her another pull and drop her on her wheels."

His hearer, his hand again to his neck, was about

to speak but Geoff reached in and carefully pulled on the hand brake of the car. Then he strode off to the truck cab. A single gentle pull and the long sports car came down easily on her offside wheels, the steep slope of the ground making the jolt inappreciable. But when he got out of the cab and returned Monsieur and Madame were waiting for him. For a little they both spoke at once. Then the lady broke off to let her husband continue. What could he say, Monsieur wanted to know? It was a brave act of the young man, with the pig of a car hanging there ready to fall upon him. And what could he say to one who had saved Madame's life and restored to him his so unfortunate neck? . . . His poor neck! Ooooo!

"Now, see here, M'sieur . . ." Geoff laughed.

"Montserrat, Henri Montserrat," the Frenchman interjected.

"Oh, Mason's my name, Geoff Mason."

The old man turned back to his wife, with the air of one about to introduce the most distinguished of all eminent persons. "*Marie, ma chère*—M'sieur Geoff!"

And it would seem that Madame had waited a lifetime to meet Monsieur Geoff. Her enthusiasm was as torrential as her French. But, watching her laughing face and eloquent hands, Geoff marvelled that a woman of her age and doubtless unused to shocks, could have an overturned car lifted off her and be able to talk at all. However, having made his acknowledgments as best he could, he managed to return to what he had intended to say earlier.

"See here, M'sieur," he said again. "We'll have a

look over your car and see what the damage is. It mightn't be so bad you know. She might have taken all her battering on her guards."

His hearer had drawn a cigar case from his pocket. He stared blankly at Geoff for a moment. Then he sprang into the air and several cigars cascaded on to the damp grass.

"Bad? Not bad, you say!" He pointed at the big blue car and spat fiercely. "It is the machine terrible! Again to drive it I will not! *Attendez*, M'sieur Geoff. I am drive over the 'ill. My cigar I cannot think where I put 'im. For one moment—one only M'sieur—I turn to search, and poof! Ze pig of a car 'e dive this side then that side. Then 'e dive from ze road and through ze barricade, what you say, ze fence. One would then surmise that is enough. *Mais non!* 'E then spring upon ze neck! I push, I pull, I try to call to Marie but will ze neck work? *Non!* And ze breathe I cannot do! *Non, non, mon ami*, I 'ave ze automobile that stay topside up and do not spring upon ze neck. 'E is, what you say, reliable. Yet I think 'e is not good enough I must 'ave ze automobile sports! Non, M'sieur, it is better sense I must 'ave! This,"—again he pointed fiercely and again he spat—"this is *auto diable*! I do not again trust 'im with *ma chère Marie* and in 'im again I do not, what you say, risk ze neck! *Non*, nevaire!"

Geoff nodded, not trusting himself to speak. Instead he stepped across to the long, low-built sports, slipped the rope from the handle of the driver's door and opened the door. The first thing he noticed was the smell of new leather. Clearly the car was brand new, just out of the showroom. He joggled the gear lever into neutral then found and pressed the starter and the engine sprang to life. He tried the gears carefully, then let in the clutch and drove the big car round on to level ground. At last he got out and spoke to the Frenchman.

"You're lucky, M'sieur. I'm game to bet there's nothing wrong with that car beyond the damaged body work. Jove, she's a lovely job and no mistake! You don't see a car in a year like her." He was laughing now. "It wasn't her fault she went into that skid. You can't go reaching for cigar butts driving on a hot bitumen road that's just had a shower on it."

He looked at the big sports again. He knew her now. She was one of the big twelve-cylinder Mintons he'd read an account of recently and he'd admired pictures of them in several papers. Cæsar, what a car! He didn't realise that the old Frenchman and his wife were watching him closely. Then suddenly he heard Madame speaking, but in French again. She spoke rapidly for more than a minute. Monsieur replied, also at length. Then Madame began again. Geoff turned away, despair in his heart. They were at it again! But he'd better do something about getting them into town. And then Monsieur had him by the arm.

"M'sieur Geoff, you have ze automobile, yes?" Geoff looked his surprise.

"Why, no, M'sieur," he grinned. "Uncle George makes out all right with the truck. As for myself . . ." Again a cry as of a lost soul burst from Monsieur but clearly it was a cry of delight.

"Then *attendez*, M'sieur Geoff!" The old man's

face was filled now with eagerness. "I 'ave talk with Marie, M'sieur. We 'ave thank you that you risk your life for us, yes. That is very well, M'sieur, if one can do no more than thank you. But attend again, M'sieur. This automobile nevaire will I drive again, *non*! Also, I am, what you say, I am well off, M'sieur. Yet this automobile of the devil, it is, it seems, to your liking. Then we implore you, M'sieur! Marie, 'e implore you, M'sieur! Already we 'ave ze auto that do not squeeze ze neck. With this machine we 'ave finish! Then, again, M'sieur Geoff, we implore you that you take 'im!" With his last word Madame was close beside him her face as eager as his own.

The brown-faced boy looked at them both and laughed heartily. "Good heavens, M'sieur, I couldn't accept a gift like that for helping two people in a crash! Why, if you don't want the car you can get nearly all your money back for her! Now, look here, we'll just get your stuff into the truck and I'll run you into town. Madame must have had about all she can stand."

But, far from becoming ill as Geoff feared, Madame took over where M'sieur had left off. Did M'sieur Geoff think they did not know he had risked his life and had acted quickly yet with great intelligence? As a result Henri, her dear husband, was still with her. But now, M'sieur Geoff, having offered his life, refused their thank-offering. That indeed was unkind, surely! Would he not understand that, to M'sieur her husband, the cost of the car was not a serious matter. Madame's face and hands expressed the same agony of entreaty, and she struggled bravely with her English. Surely M'sieur Geoff could see how it would grieve them if he refused the automobile so abominable!

The argument that followed lasted half an hour. Two cars came over the hill and slowed down while their drivers looked hard and passed on, convinced from the vigour of Madame's and Monsieur gestures, that the smash had ended not in tragedy but in a first-class row and they'd better stay out of it. Geoff refused to accept the Minton. He repeated his refusal. He refused a third and a fourth time. Then he found himself looking helplessly into Madame's tear-stained face.

Three hours later he stood on Murundy railway station and watched the Brisbane train steam out. He stood and waved his handkerchief. Then he returned to Jake Hawkins's garage to find a big sports car having her crumpled mudguards hammered out and a temporary windscreen fitted. His uncle's truck stood in the yard. He frowned in surprise.

"Hang it, Jake," he said to the owner, "I didn't think you'd be starting on this job right away. The fact is I'd like to leave her in your shop for a bit. You see . . ." But Jake Hawkins shook his head.

"Be glad if you'd take her away, Geoff, that's why I put the boys straight on to her. We can knock the guards into shape well enough to make it safe to drive her and fix up the windscreen a bit but we can't finish her—just haven't got the gear for work like this. And . . . well, we're packed up with work, Geoff, and she's too expensive to leave out in the yard."

The fact was that, though Geoff had finally succumbed to Madame's tears, he found himself still confused about the whole affair and he had a hazy idea of leaving the big car with Jake Hawkins till he had talked the matter over with his uncle. But it almost seemed as if all and sundry were determined that the big Minton was to be his. He hesitated for the last time, then grinned.

"Okay, Jake, I'll take her away as soon as you've done with her. Jim Gordon's in town with his dad. He'll drive Uncle's truck home and I'll slip over to his place and get it to-morrow."

In his pocket was the card of Henri Montserrat, Jewel Merchant, Brisbane, and he had made the old Frenchman a solemn promise that he would not pass through Brisbane without calling on him and Madame.

"For then, perhaps, ze neck 'e will be 'eal," Monsieur had chuckled huskily, framed in the window of the railway carriage, one hand waving a cigar, the other caressing the doctor's bandages under his ears. "And remember, *mon ami*, if ze job you 'ave not got, *tous les jours* I 'ave one for you, *mais oui*!"

"Remember!" Madame laughed, and kissed him as the train began to move.

CHAPTER THREE

THE FIRE

THE STOREKEEPER carefully lowered a package into a big carton. He ticked off an item on a docket and, with a dexterous flick of the wrist, tore the docket cleanly from the book. He smiled across the counter at Geoff.

"That's the lot, Geoff."

His hearer put out a hand and drew the carton towards him. "Thanks, Mr. Green. This should keep us ticking another week. Well, I guess I'll push off."

"Well, now, I was coming to that, Geoff. Your uncle rang up about two o'clock, just after you dropped in the grocery order. He says the windmill pump plunger has stripped its thread and he's rung Treloars. They haven't got one of that model but Mick Treloar's turning an old Cartwright plunger to fit. It won't be ready till pretty late as he has to finish an urgent job first. Your uncle says will you have tea in town and collect the plunger when it's done."

"Oh, okay," Geoff grinned. "I'm having quite a day out! I'll just shove round to Treloar's and see what's doing. Well, good night, and thanks again, Mr. Green."

He picked up the heavy carton of groceries, strode

out of the shop door and put them in the boot of the big Minton, drawn up at the kerb. Then he got in and drove round to the machinery agents. The plunger, he found, would not be finished for an hour and he came back to Tanner's Café and ordered a grill.

When he got away at last the summer sunlight was already gone. The big twelve cylinder sports purred along with a silky smoothness he had never thought possible in any car and, her headlights splashing the road ahead with white light, the eleven miles out to the farm were soon behind him. Opposite the farm he swung her off the road and drew up at an iron gate. As she gathered speed again from the gate, her powerful lights lit the farm track leading up to the house, flinging long pivoting shadows from the fence posts. And then something beyond the white light caught his attention. He leant over the wheel to look again. Next moment the big car was leaping ahead under wide throttle, the fence posts flicking past faster and faster. At the end of the fence there was another gate. Geoff skidded the car to a halt, leapt out, vaulted the gate and was running for the farmhouse fifty yards beyond.

As he ran, his eyes were on a red glare pouring from the window of his uncle's bedroom. Two bounds took him up the front steps, then he was across the veranda, through the front door and in the smoke-filled doorway of his uncle's room. He crouched and peered as he shouted.

"Uncle! . . . Uncle George!"

The kerosene lamp was lying on its side, a pillar of

flame from its spilled contents reaching for the varnished boards of the ceiling; but already two walls were blazing and crackling. Blinded by smoke and the glare, Geoff paused a moment longer, then plunged through the smoke to his uncle's bed. It was still made and empty. Then, just when the heat seemed more than he could endure, he saw a bulky figure slumped against the farther wall. In a moment he had slipped a strong hand under each armpit and, with a powerful lift, swung the inert form across his shoulders. He staggered a little in the smoke of the doorway. Then he was out in the moonlight.

He lowered his burden to the grass and knelt quickly beside it. As he did a tongue of flame burst from the window and the prone figure was suddenly in bright yellow light. The lad drew a sharp breath. An ugly gash showed from the right temple to the cheek bone, the blood from it coursing in a glittering rivulet down the cheek and neck to stain the open shirt. The skull on the side near the wound had clearly been struck a savage blow! But who would attack George Warburton, one of the kindest men alive? Only a thug would do that, someone trying to rob him.

Geoff ripped a sleeve from his shirt and made a thick bandage that would stanch the wound at least. His next thought was of brandy. But the flames had worked as swiftly as he. It was a pine-built house and old, for the farm was old when his uncle had bought it four years ago. The pine walls and ceiling, after weeks of summer heat, were so much tinder. The fire had roared both ways along the hall and now smoke poured from every door and window and the heat was unbearable at thirty yards distance. The flame that had first burst from a window was playing like a giant blowlamp upon a rain tank beside it and already the water in the tank was boiling madly. There was no question of getting back into that inferno! The roaring in his ears, Geoff looked desperately right and left along the hillside; but he looked in vain. His big sports car stood down beyond the gate. From through the house fence, a saddle-marked brown gelding faced him, head erect, his long shadow wavering behind him. In the red light he looked a grotesque from another world. But that was all. Hansfield's place was screened by the hump of the hill. They might not have noticed the fire yet.

When he looked down his uncle's eyes flickered open and they were filled with the most intense eagerness Geoff had ever seen in any man's eyes. He bent close, inwardly cursing the crackling roar of the fire. But, with his ear almost touching the moving lips, he caught the few words they spoke.

"Wanted you have farm, Geoff . . . but forgot will . . . perhaps find limestone ridge . . . started draw map . . . Graster got wrong box. . . ." The whispering stopped for it seemed that all the injured man's will and strength had gone into those slowly gasped words. Geoff could see him fighting for enough strength to speak again. But it was not to be. The eyes flickered and closed; the powerful form relaxed and slumped against him.

His uncle was dead.

Sometime later, he did not know how long, the boy got to his feet. Beyond the fence the old brown saddle-marked gelding still stood watching the fire, his shadow flung far behind him down the grassy slope.

CHAPTER FOUR

THE INQUEST

George Warburton had been father and mother to Geoff since both the youngster's parents had been killed in a motor smash twelve years ago. And now his uncle had been murdered. Of that he was bitterly certain. But the days that followed were mercifully full. His Aunt Hester, George Warburton's only sister, came on the first available train from Sydney and Geoff met her and settled her in a hotel in town. Then there were the funeral arrangements . . . and the inquest.

At the inquest, Geoff gave it as his opinion that the injury to his uncle had been the result of a savage attack and related how Warburton had tried to tell him about a man he called Graster having stolen a brief box. The coroner heard him out, saying nothing. When the last witness had been stood down, however, he sat looking before him, one hand nervously arranging a little pile of papers. Then he called Geoff again into the stand.

"What is your aunt's name, Geoff?" he asked quietly.

"Her name? . . . Why . . . she is Miss Warburton, sir. . . . Miss Hester Warburton."

"And that is what I wish you to note, Geoff. Her name is Hester. And she would, don't you think, have been in your uncle's thoughts before he died.

I feel certain it was her name he spoke 'Hester.' You admit that the fire was roaring and it was difficult for you to hear your uncle's words. I will go further and say I do not think you heard clearly anything he said and I repeat I believe that the name you hear was 'Hester' not 'Graster.' Police investigation has failed to reveal any evidence whatever of foul play, for the injuries could, from the doctor's finding, have resulted from a fall. I declare that, in the opinion of this court, death resulted from accidental causes."

So that was it! Geoff thought. The police had found nothing to support his opinion that his uncle had been done to death. But their failure and the coroner's finding left him unshaken in his belief. He made no further comment, however, and, when he had left the stand, the court rose. He walked back to the hotel with his aunt. There was, he knew, one more matter to be settled.

Two weeks ago he had come back from working on a boring plant that had just finished a contract of five shafts on Timor Station. He had always come to the farm for his school holidays for had it not always been his home. More than that, his uncle had several times told him that the farm would be his. But his uncle had left no will! It was the old story, with which lawyers are only too familiar, of a man, intelligent and in every way considerate, putting off a small task that, once done, would save much injustice. As for the farm it would go now to Warburton's sister along with some ten thousand pounds invested and in the bank. And Aunt Hester, Geoff knew, had never liked him and believed he had already had far too much assistance from his uncle. She would offer him no part of either farm or money. Indeed her words left no room for doubt.

"I have already had a solicitor's advice, Geoff, and he can arrange with the Public Trustee for a manager to take over the farm to-morrow. Of course there is no need for you to hurry away...."

His eyes met hers scornfully.

"Thank you, Aunt, to-morrow will suit me very well," he said.

CHAPTER FIVE

THE ATTACK

BACK AT the hotel, after seeing his aunt off on the Sydney train, Geoff found Jack Green waiting for him, and the kindly storekeeper insisted upon taking him home for the evening. Two of Green's sons worked in the store. Green himself talked cheerfully and finally led the conversation round to water boring. The boys asked Geoff many questions.

"I can't make out why some of the bigger properties round here haven't got the big gushers you hear of," Jim Green said. "Instead of that they seem to be satisfied with shallow shafts they have to pump the water up from."

"Well I don't know everything about underground water," Geoff replied, "but I think we're too far east here for the gushers. We're off the artesian basin altogether. The only underground water these properties can tap is not artesian but sub-artesian. That's a misleading word because it doesn't mean 'below artesian' at all. You see you don't, as a rule, have to go down more than a few hundred feet for sub-artesian water but it has to be pumped up. On the other hand the real artesian water nearly always lies deep. As you probably know, a lot of the bores in Queensland are half a mile deep. One is a mile and a half. That's a pretty deep shaft and pretty expensive to drill. But (due mostly to hydraulic pressure and sometimes to CO_2 generated at pressure by the heat down under) the water spouts up. But even out over the artesian basin they get sub-artesian water at shallow depths. A lot of the cattle-men prefer to sink a number of sub-bores rather than risk going deep and finding themselves with only a deep expensive shaft and no water after all. A dud artesian hole has bankrupted more than one grazier. But, hang it, look here, you fellows don't want a lecture on the subject, I reckon." He laughed and stood up. "I guess it's time I shoved off back to the pub."

But, back in the hot hotel room, the boy knew he was too restless to sleep. He sat on the bed a few minutes then got up, switched off the light and went down to his car. Presently the big Minton was purring along the road to the farm. He had no definite reason for going out to the farm, for he had been out and seen to the stock in the morning. As he drove, his thoughts seemed to grow more confused. In spite of his assurance to his aunt, he had scarcely considered immediate plans. There'd be some clothes to buy for most of his clothes had gone in the fire. Well, a few clothes wouldn't break him. He had some savings, thank goodness, and he had this fine car.

He drew the Minton to a stop before the farm gate, got out briskly and opened the gate, then drove through. But, as he drove on up towards the sheds a thought came to him. . . . It was fat-headed, of course. Yet there just might be something left after all! Uncle George had certainly wanted to tell him something; something about a box and a map he'd started to draw. Graster had got the wrong box! That probably meant that one of his uncle's two brief boxes had been left in the fire. He'd often seen them, both made of light iron or steel. But even a steel box would be actually burnt in that fire and even if it weren't its contents would certainly be cinders. . . . Still, it wouldn't take long to look.

He clambered over a tangle of burnt roofing iron, burnt to a papery thinness in which his boots made jagged holes at every step. He finally got down into the shallow crater in the debris and ashes where the police had worked. They had used shovels. In the days since, the loose ashes had slid back. He checked carefully to fix the position of his uncle's bedroom. Yes, that would be it. But, with half the space cleared, they had found nothing that wasn't burnt to a cinder and had given over the search. The place where his uncle had had his writing desk was covered now with a sheet of greyish black corrugated iron that curved over like a large meat cover. Then he remembered. This was not a piece of roof iron at all, but the travelling steel top of the writing desk. He stood still a moment looking down at it. Funny Uncle George having a writing desk at all, for he detested anything to do with writing. The fact was, however, he used the desk more as a cupboard for all manner of odds and ends and, of course, for storing important business papers. Then the boy leaned forward, for he dimly discerned something more in the weak moonlight. By some trick of burning timbers, one of the rain tanks, its wooden stand collapsing sideways, must have gushed its boiling contents over everything in this corner. The mark of the slopping water across the steel of the desk top was apparent by the difference in colour. Where the water had not reached it, at one end, the slats were blackened and burnt to fragile rods. But the rest of it was still sound and even strong.

Geoff put both hands to one edge and lifted. The cover came up, sending a cloud of ash into the air; and at once he exclaimed softly. Before him, as though placed there by his uncle or else fallen through the bottom of the lowest drawer, was one of the two steel brief boxes he knew.

But his hopes died when he grasped it, for two of its soldered corners had melted open. It was easy to lever back the top and he peered in. There were three compartments. Two were empty. In the third was a folded sheet, charred at its folded corner.

With an ash-soiled hand the boy dragged out his wallet and arranged it as a wrapper round the charred sheet, finally thrusting the whole again into his pocket. It was as well he did. He was turning again to the brief box when a crash came from just behind him. He wheeled to find a man sprawled in the debris. The man regained his feet like a cat and sprang straight at Geoff but, as he lunged, the slight-built lad met him with a swift upper cut. He pitched over sideways and lay with his face to the sky; but at the same moment a voice cried "Come on Dirk!" and two men came leaping over the ruins as the man Geoff had knocked down sat up. Geoff had to think fast. Three to one! Better get out of this tangle of rubbish to begin with.

In half a dozen leaps the youngster was clear of the twisted tin and ashes. Then he decided to jump the side fence and meet his assailants as they came over. He reached the picket fence but as he vaulted it, a hand on a post, there came the staccato bark of an automatic and a bullet zipped from beside his hand on the top of the post. The murdering swine! Automatics! He'd just have to outrun these birds! He sprang away along the picket fence, stooping lower down, vaulted it and was on his way again, running hard down the easy slope. Automatics! Gosh, if he had a gun he'd play that game too, confound them! He flung a glance behind him. Two of the men were all he could see. Apparently the pace was too hard for the third. . . . Then he heard the same voice again.

"Let him have it, Dirk, curse him!" The automatic spoke again, this time in a burst of three shots. All three whipped past within inches—all misses but good shooting for all that! This swine was a killer and a practised gunman! Geoff felt his anger mounting but he fought it down and changed his run to a zigzagging. A couple more bursts like that one! . . . and suddenly the moon slipped behind a thick cloud.

In a moment Geoff changed his direction, bearing left and putting all his strength into a sprint. The Hansfields might hear the shots perhaps but their house was well over the rise. No, the railway cutting was his best chance now. Then the moon flashed out once more and, with the light, came a shouted oath and another burst of shots. But his sprint and swing left had gained him distance and only one came close. Better still, with a gasp of relief, he saw a railway cutting two hundred yards ahead. He kept on till he had halved the distance, then glanced back. The gunman had jerked to a stop and dropped on one knee and he was aiming carefully!

Geoff threw himself down. As he did he felt a hot sting in his right arm, but now he was scuffling on hands and knees. Three bullets zipped wickedly from the ground where he had fallen and he knew that only the uncertain light had saved him once again. He sprang up and commenced a zigzag run but he was about to drop once more when he saw the cutting's edge right before him. He was over it in a stride, not knowing or caring how far he would fall. His feet jarred on the gritty bottom of a narrow ditch beside railway sleepers.

The cutting was short and deep, one of many in that tumbled range country. Geoff raced along beside the line right to the eastern end and then, without crossing the tracks, he flung down, panting hoarsely, in the wider grassy ditch that dipped down beside an embankment. Next moment he heard both his pursuers reach the spot he had jumped down from. They paused there a second only, then slithered into the cutting. Above the scrabbling of their boots Geoff heard a long-drawn growl and the rhythmic coughing of an engine pulling all out.

While he lay panting, his thoughts raced on. This was the very crest of the low range. From the farm he had often watched the trains toiling over this last grade before gathering speed down the western side. A train took minutes to crawl through this cutting. That train down the slope—it would be the Western Mail; she'd be just round the next curve now, climbing slowly. If only his murderous attackers crossed the line he would have precious minutes with the train between him and them.

He put his hand to his right arm while he listened to the pounding exhaust growing steadily louder. His short shirt sleeve was edged with blood but the wound was no more than a deep cut after all. Good! And a good thing his shirt was blue—hard to see at night. At that moment a broad beam of light flung across the ravine beyond the tracks and began pivoting slowly towards him, farther and farther round till it was full in his eyes and the towering front of the toiling engine was in full view and its thundering noise was round him. Then his heart leapt as, resisting the temptation to raise his head, he looked back and saw two forms dart across the rail tracks, their faces ghastly white in the engine's searchlight. In ten seconds now, the iron monster would be between him and his assailants. The engine's siren broke into its hoarse growl while the pounding staccato of her exhaust flung far and wide. But in that instant with the engine already abreast of Geoff, his pursuers came springing back again, thirty yards beyond her!

It was too late now for Geoff to cross the line himself. One desperate glance showed him the first carriage, its window lights splashing the roadside. As it glided slowly up beside him he drew up his legs and tensed . . . then he sprang through the moving-light squares into the blackness beside the carriage. He glimpsed a stab of flame from the ditch but the thunder of the engine drowned the shot. He put two hands to a long board that was gliding past him, the ladder board, some four inches wide under the carriage. He swung lengthwise along it, far back in the train's black shadow. There was a chance that, looking through the glare flung out by the windows, the killers might lose sight of him. They might think he was running back along the train.

The next five seconds seemed like long minutes. To lie prone and helpless and expect every instant a burst of bullets crashing through him! He could see the bright light squares gliding slowly with him. . . . But no shots came. Instead, he watched, fascinated, while the tip of a slow-gliding light square seemed to climb over two crouching forms, their faces peering back towards the rear of the train. . . . The swine had lost sight of him! He'd made it! He was past them! The carriage had swung the curve!

And now, once over the crown of the hill, the engine's vast weight tilted down grade and was aiding her full-throttle pulling. Again her siren sounded a primeval growl and she began at once to gather speed. At once Geoff's narrow board began to sway. He moved his hands in search of a firmer grip, winding his legs round the board. But a lurch and then another told him it would not do. Once the train had gained speed he would most certainly be thrown off. He must risk jumping off now or get a grip of something else. He screwed and looked up. There was a window just above him. His mouth set grimly. Then he drew up his feet, hunched himself a moment on feet and one hand, then straightened, lunging outwards and upwards. His right hand, outstretched, just caught the window ledge. The wrench sent a stabbing pain up his arm and all but tore away his grasp. Already, in those few seconds, the train was swaying. He looked back and saw that it was completely over the crest of the hill. The steep grade seemed to add speed with every yard.

Then the siren growled again, there came a fire-hot wind gust and all in a moment, the world was an inferno of smoke, steam and flickering lights, lights that flickered in the midst of ear-splitting noise!

The tunnel! He had forgotten. the tunnel that pierced the opposite bank of the ravine! . . . Still panting hard from his all-out run, he had suddenly only steam-filled smoke to breathe! A great weight clamped round his lungs and faintness smothered his brain. The flickering lights went out, leaving him only darkness and acrid heat and the terrible weight upon his lungs. Already they seemed to be bursting. He could feel his fingers slipping . . . slipping from the window ledge!

But a hand he could not see gripped his wrist and a great arm closed like a vice about his shoulders. . . . Five seconds later he was lying, full-stretch, on a carriage seat.

CHAPTER SIX

THE MAP

EARLY DAYLIGHT filled the rattling carriage. Geoff Mason leant back in a corner seat and looked at a red-headed English lad of his own age, whose gloomy expression was strangely belied by a pair of dare-devil eyes. The youngster shook his red head sadly and spoke.

"Well, it's the queerest show I've heard of," he said. "In the middle of a law-abiding farm district a bloke has to bolt for it with automatic bullets chipping bits off him. But don't misunderstand me, feller. I know a tough when I see one and *you* don't look the part. What's more, you've told a straight story and shown me that map as well."

Geoff laughed. "About the least I could do, considering I've had my life saved. But you haven't taken much interest in the map. . . ."

"None of my business, son," the other said curtly. "But it's a queer show, as I said. You'd better give up thinking about it for a bit. You're in poor shape for solving mysteries, in spite of being put out cold for six hours by the dose of brandy Dogfoot poured into you."

A well-knit lad of scarcely medium height, Geoff's gloomy, red-headed acquaintance had introduced himself an hour ago as "Blue" Campbell. He sat opposite Geoff now, right elbow on his knee, and scowled in thought. But, as though Geoff had not brought enough with him to think about already, he had found himself face to face with a boy he had seen before; seen only once, but that once was enough. Months ago, at the Sydney Royal Show he had been one of a crowd looking down into a circular wooden pit and had watched this English youngster ride a roaring motor-bicycle round and round the vertical walls, the bike roaring with wide open throttle, clinging like a giant beetle half-way up those sheer walls, racing round and round the pit's circumference . . . half-way up, three-quarters up the wall . . . finally roaring madly round and round within a hair-raising foot of the top. At last, having diced with death, the madman had eased the throttle, spiralled the big bike down the circular wall to the floor and stopped it. Then he had pulled his crash-helmet off his flaring red hair, made a single quick salute in acknowledgment of the crowd's clamour and stepped through a little door out of sight.

That same poker face under the shock of red hair was before Geoff now.

The only other occupant of the compartment was a blackfellow; but one of the biggest men Geoff had ever seen. It was he who had seen and caught him, and dragged him out of the inferno of the tunnel. He sat forward now, hands on knees, watching the speeding landscape with the wide eyes of a child, his vast arms thrust out of his coat sleeves. Geoff watched him a moment. There was something laughably contradictory about those child-like eyes looking out of a bearded face that was the face of a hunter, firm-set and dignified. Then Geoff turned back to Blue Campbell.

"I'm darned glad to have come across you again, Blue."

Blue Campbell nodded gloomily: "I'm darned glad to be here to be come across," he answered. "I got what was coming to me the day before the Show finished;—a crack-up—bike on top of me, unconscious for a week, cracked skull, two broken ribs, broken leg. I'm fixed again, but the smash stimulated my brain a bit."

"Gosh! That was a bad business right enough!"

"Oh, you've got to expect it in that game. My boss and I were making £200 a week each. It's a grand way to earn a living. The only trouble is you don't live long. I got out alive and, believe me, I'm going to stay out. . . . Hallo!" He glanced quickly out the window. "We'll be in Gundaloo in less than half an hour. That's where Dogfoot and I pull out. What about you? You still only look about five per cent. How about getting off and having some breakfast with us? That should help."

Geoff was grinning now.

"Well, I guess the sooner I get off this train and into one going in the opposite direction the better," he said. "Good thing I've got enough money with me for fares or I'd be finishing at the police station. I'm with you, son, if you can stand me a bit longer."

Blue Campbell nodded and for the first time he grinned. He twisted and addressed the giant blackfellow: "Catchem breakfast plenty soon. Catchem swag quick-fellow!"

The black replied in a voice deep and rich that boomed above the train's skirling. "Okay Boss. Him close up hot day too much!"

He stood up and reached down two big suitcases with the ease most people would lift down small parcels. Tossed on the carriage seat, their weight pressed deep into the cushions. Geoff watched in amazement. Those great arms had saved his life last night. This man had the strength of two. But the pidgin English? Hang it, the blacks down south-east here spoke like any other Aussie. Certainly none spoke pidgin. As if to answer his thoughts Blue Campbell, tightening a shoe-lace, jerked his head at the big black.

"Dogfoot's a bit of a curiosity down here in the south-east. He's a long way from his own stamping ground. But I had to fetch him with me for the simple reason that he wouldn't stay behind. The fact is, I was out in Western Queensland and came on the son of a gun in trouble with a station manager bloke and the police. They actually had him man-acled and on his way to the quarter sessions for cattle-spearing. Things looked as bad for him as they could, and the beggar knew it. But I'd happened on a bit of evidence in my travels and proved he was as innocent as anybody could be. The police didn't hesitate when they heard what I knew and they turned him loose then and there. But then the real trouble started. Believe it or not the big lumbering codger reckons I'm very nearly the only thing in Queensland worth mentioning. I talked myself blind, but I might as well have tried to persuade a gate post. I said I was going right back east to the coast. Okay, he points east and says that's where he's going. I said I was coming south. So then he points south and says he's going there too. Since then he's fixed my boots, does all the washing and ironing and mends my blessed socks, even. *Darns* 'em, mind you. If I'd let him he'd pluck my blessed eyebrows and tell me bedtime stories!"

Geoff chuckled delightedly, glanced at the big black, eagerly watching the paddock fences wheeling past, then grinned at the speaker.

"You mean he's a real cook? How the devil did he learn to cook and launder and mend socks?"

"Well, it seems he was laid up at a station homestead for six weeks with a broken thigh bone and used the time watching the cook and the laundry team. But he can get round in a city, too. He can go to any place in Brisbane if he's been there once. He knows the streets by the buildings and marks on the roadway and things like that and the beggar's got a memory second only to Einstein's. As for cleanliness, I threatened him if he didn't bath twice a week and wash three times a day I'd have him arrested and sent north. So the old gazooker baths four or five times a week and washes his neck and ears every two hours to be on the safe side. . . . Hallo, this looks like the blister they call Gundaloo. And, by gum, Dogfoot's pretty right. She's going to be a scorcher of a day. All up too hot!"

The train slowed into the station and the trio alighted.

"Murundy, eh?" the night officer said, to Geoff at the exit barrier. "You must have boarded the old girl in a deuce of a hurry!"

"I was in a bigger hurry than that," Geoff grinned.

The other made a noise that was somewhere between a cheerful grunt and a sympathetic snort.

"Well, Murundy's a hundred and fifty miles from here. You could have saved a quid by saying you came from a nearer town. Anyhow, you don't look the sort of bloke the police would chase on to a train."

Geoff's face was cold sober as he replied. "No, the police didn't chase me on to it. But I've got to go back to-day. What time does Swooping Sally pull out of here?"

The night officer grinned. "So that's what you call her along your way? She's known as Lazy Lou out here. Aw, she's due to pull out at 11.16 but she's never been known to. Still, you can't tell with Lou, she might up and surprise you. One morning she got away in such a hurry she blew half her funnel a couple of hundred feet into the air and it fell through the roof of old Ah Took's shop and into an egg box. Some of the eggs got broke."

In the general laugh, Geoff gathered his change and they walked into the already hot roadway behind the station.

"Know the town?" Blue asked. "No? Well, the Federal's not a bad old pub. Just over there. Dad and Mum and I stayed there three years ago when we first came out to Australia.

The proprietor looked hard at the big blackfellow when they entered the hotel but apparently he knew Blue Campbell and what that worthy had to say satisfied him. He took them up to a big balcony room.

"Bathe the body and comb the hair. Here we go!" Blue said gloomily. He whipped up the lid of one of the big suitcases Dogfoot had set on the floor and rummaged for soap and towels.

An hour later, and breakfast over, the three strolled out on to the balcony that opened from their room. Dogfoot went straight to the railing and leant upon it.

"Well, I feel a lot better for all that," Geoff laughed. He glanced at his watch. "I'll have to wire my hotel in Murundy at nine, but my train's not due for over two hours yet."

Blue Campbell looked gloomily along the hot street below them. "My dad's in the show business but I'm out of it for good, as I told you. I'm doing a bit of roaming around at present and I came up here to see about a job on a boring plant. All I know about boring for water could be written on a postage stamp but looking at the boring plants at the Sydney Show, it seems to me it'd be an interesting business. Anyhow I thought I'd give this chap's outfit a look over."

"Hang it, now, that's interesting!" Geoff rejoined quickly. "The fact is, I've been working on a boring plant myself."

Some of the gloom vanished from Blue Campbell's face. "You don't say! Then you're the very chap I want to talk to. Do you think . . . well, would you come out with me and look over this show for me? The boring plant's supposed to be out on Carmen Station, about eight miles from town. I'll guarantee to have you back in time for your train."

"Why, sure, if that's how you feel," Geoff answered. "You're welcome to my advice for what it's worth, which won't be much, I'm warning you."

Blue rang for a taxi and within an hour they were climbing out of it beside a shallow-boring outfit right in the middle of a treeless station paddock. The plant was not working, however, and there was no one about. They had been told at the station homestead that the owner was in town and that they could have found him any time in the last week in the bar of the Welland hotel.

The appearance of the outfit certainly didn't inspire any desire to know its owner after all, and Blue Campbell's face resumed its thoughtful gloom as he and Geoff walked round the battered drilling tower. The engine was heeled over crazily in her chocks, the struts of the tower were loose and sagging and there were empty oil tins and tangles of rusty steel cables all round. A big, broken drill stem lay untidily beside several drills so badly burred they couldn't be said to have an edge left at all. Geoff stepped to the top of the bore shaft and glanced up at the top of the tower, then ducked under the eccentric bar and examined the cable run on the drum. From there he looked thoughtfully at the unseated engine. Finally he looked at Blue and laughed.

"I don't think you need any advice about this show, feller. In the first place, whoever owns it seems to be just boggling along and, by the look of the engine bounced out of her bed he's had trouble—jammed gear. But you can see for yourself the plant's finished. There's always plenty of worry, even with a good plant. A bad one makes boring a first-class nightmare. If you took a job with this chap you'd be lucky to get your pay, I reckon."

Blue nodded, unsmiling. "Somehow I keep trying to get rich the hard way! Well, we'd better get out of here before the contraption falls on us."

They were back in the hotel by ten o'clock.

"Look here, Blue," Geoff said as they strolled out on the balcony again. "Now you've had the benefit of my master mind, how about taking a look at this map of mine for me? I haven't made any plans yet, to tell you the truth. I know what I want to do but whether I can do it depends on what I can make out from this scrap of paper. Now, you've been out in Western Queensland, and you might know something about the piece of it in the map."

The English lad nodded and grinned. "Okay I'll take a look, feller."

"Fine!"

Geoff drew his wallet from his pocket again, opened it with the utmost care and spread the half-charred sheet of paper on a small table near the doorway. Still with extreme care he weighted down all four corners with a two-shilling piece to each. The two boys looked down at the discoloured sheet. This is what they saw:

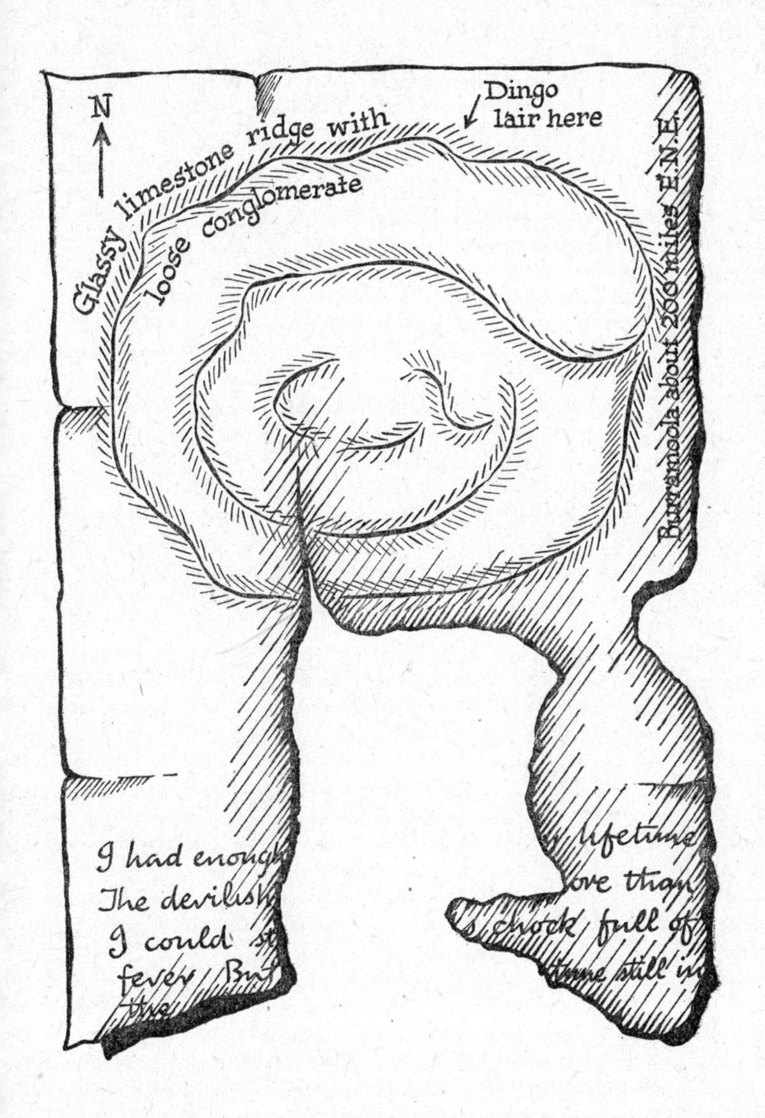
N
Glassy limestone ridge with
loose conglomerate
Dingo
lair here
Burramoola about 200 miles E.N.E.
I had enough
The devilish
I could st
fever But
the
lifetime
ove than
s chock full of
time still in

The longer he studied the rough sketch map the more convinced Geoff became that it was unfinished—just the beginning of a map. In the first place, that was typical of Uncle George. Writing anything had always exasperated him. He had begun to make a map, jotted down a few notes then impatiently put it aside. Still, that may not have been the whole story. He may, for instance, have been trying to remember; trying to recall details. But now here was all there was—this rough-drawn map; and even some of *it* was missing for two edges of the sheet and a part of one end were burnt away and some of the rest charred to a blackish brown, almost obliterating the pencilled letters. For several minutes neither lad spoke. Then Blue shook his head gloomily.

"Just enough to make you wonder," he said. "A limestone ridge, to begin with, 200 miles from Burramoola. I know where Burramoola is, but, heck, there's hundreds of miles of limestone ridges out beyond there, they tell me, and devil's country it is, by all accounts. I've heard some prospector chaps say it's the most useless formation known to man as far as minerals are concerned. They're short ridges, just bare rock, and there could be a thousand of 'em. Your uncle has picked one with a crevice in it used by dingoes for a lair! To identify this ridge of his you'd have to find that crevice. There *might* be tracks but limestone can be darned hard as you know, and he calls it glassy. There's dingoes out there right enough, but if they holed up in the ridge country it would have to be on the edge of it, I'd say, because it's waterless. But, about these notes at the bottom of the map. Take the first line:

"'*I had enough . . . my lifetime.*' Enough of what?"

Geoff frowned in thought. "Well, Blue, Uncle George never seemed to want to talk about himself but I know that, up till four years ago he made a living from prospecting. Apparently he made sufficient to get by; for one thing he kept me at school when the money my dad left ran out. He was years in the north and north-west and in Western Australia, too, chasing gold and tin and opals and manganese and anything else he came on prospects of. But after his last trip, a little over four years ago, he came back south-east and bought the farm."

Blue nodded. "Looks as though he got out that last time with a pretty decent swag of something, then—gold, probably; enough to buy a farm and give up prospecting. But something funny must have happened on that last trip. Apparently he only *just* got out. For one thing he must have been in a bad way with malaria. And there's this bit: '*but . . . tune still in the* . . .' That's obvious enough as far as it goes. He reckons there's a fortune still there where he made his find. Just where that was, is going to be your worry, feller."

Geoff shook his head. "Uncle had something on his mind, Blue. He started to note down some information. But he must have been nearly too sick to see, when he left that ridge of his and, quite likely, he'd be hazy later on, very hazy, as to its whereabouts. But Graster and company are prepared to commit murder to get hold of what information he had. And the rest of the notes make it clear that there was, as you say, something darned queer connected with that gold find, Blue; something that, sick like he was, very nearly beat Uncle George. It may have been that he just managed to get clear of Graster but finally managed to throw the swine off his trail."

"Looks like it at that," Blue agreed. "And, for all we know, Graster might have spent a long time looking for him in Western Australia instead of New South Wales. Anyhow, in the end he found him; but you've got the information he wants. That's why he set his tough lad on to you with an automatic—the chap he called Dirk."

With a movement that was almost savage, Geoff leant forward, the knuckles of both hands on the table and though his voice was low it was very angry.

"The swine murdered the best friend I had, Blue. That they murdered him I'm absolutely certain. Some of the story's out there in Western Queensland. I'm going there to see what I can find out."

A car drew nearer then stopped in the street below and when it did the balcony was silent. The big blackfellow stood leaning on the rail as he had been doing the whole time. The silence lasted perhaps five seconds. Then Blue looked keenly at Geoff.

"How about the police?"

Geoff shook his head. "They're great chaps and

if I thought I could convince them I'd go to them straight. But the trouble is they already think I'm seeing and hearing things that aren't there. I need more evidence. Either I'll find it out in those ridges, or else Graster will risk showing his hand once too often, the hound. If I'm still on deck then, that will be the time to go to the police."

Blue nodded, his eyes on Geoff's face. Again there was silence. Then Blue leant forward, the glare from the hot street beyond the balcony showing up his lean face and red hair.

"Well, now, Geoff, I'll just say this. I reckon I've got to be a restless beggar. I suppose being in the show business with Dad and Mum has made me a bit that way. Anyhow Dad says if I must roam around I might as well do so, and get it out of my system. Well, I've learnt a bit about Western Queensland for one thing. So . . . well, you might want a mate on this trip of yours. Then again you might rather go by yourself. If so, that's okay with me and there'll be no hard feelings. But if not, I'd like to come with you, sharing expenses and sharing what we find. As I said, it's a suggestion and no offence if it doesn't suit you."

Geoff looked from the keen face with its steady eyes to the giant blackfellow at the balcony rail. Then suddenly he was grinning at the speaker.

"You're dead right about my wanting a mate, Blue, and I'd be darned glad to have you. As for a share of what we find, you can see for yourself it's likely to be trouble and not much else. Still there's a chance we *will* find something better. If so, we'll share alike. If you bring Dogfoot he'll be taking pretty much the same risks as we will and I owe him a lot already. If we find something good I'm agreeable to split it three ways. What do you say?"

Blue's answer was to hold out his hand. Geoff grinned and gripped it and they shook hands across the little charred map on the table between them.

CHAPTER SEVEN

A QUEST BEGINS

THE DIM shed reverberated to the roar of a twelve cylinder engine revved high. Then the roar changed to a purr and finally to a contented whispering, scarcely audible at all. It ceased when Geoff, a sandal-shod foot thrust out to the running board of his Minton reached and switched off the ignition.

"Hmph! Not so bad. Like a new engine!" Blue Campbell spoke from the glare of the doorway. Geoff laughed and turned to the big blackfellow standing a yard away.

"What do *you* think Dogfoot?" Then he turned to Blue: "*Like* a new engine? She *is* a new engine." Upon which he told Blue briefly of the roadside incident, being careful to make no mention of the risk he'd taken. Blue stepped inside the shed and listened without comment. When Geoff had finished he spoke without smiling:

"What you're telling me is that you picked a fellow up out of the ditch and he gave you this car," he growled. "Just a nice little bedtime story. But I know Frenchmen a bit as a matter of fact. They're very polite but they're not fools. So either you did something more for that chap than you've told me or else you pinched his car. Since it's a nice morning I'm giving you the benefit of the doubt." He turned back to the big sports.

"Hmph!" he said again. "When you said yesterday you owned a Minton I just reckoned you were having a little joke, that what you did own was an old bus you were calling a Minton for fun. And, from the doorway there and with the duco off the panels and guards and the patched-up windscreen she looked a bit like a bomb." His face was full of interest now. "I can see now what she is." He paused, seeming deliberately to suppress the note of excitement in his voice. "Well, I think you said you were taking Mr. Everett over the farm. Okay, you run along. I'll get your bus out and have her ready to drive away when you come back."

The trio had arrived in Murundy the night before and had come out to the farm this morning after breakfast. A man named Everett was there, camped in the machinery shed. He was the man Miss Warburton had engaged to manage the farm. He had sent word to the hotel the previous day that he had found Geoff's car near the house and had run her into a shed; by which time the hotel had had a 'phone call from Geoff. Geoff greeted him civilly, much to his relief and when the lad offered to go round the farm with him he had been very pleased, for the more you know about a particular farm the more you can get out of it. Especially is it necessary to know the differences of soil and slope and the winter herbage to be expected in this paddock and that.

"Okay, then, thanks, feller," Geoff said in reply to Blue's offer to get the Minton out and await his return. He picked up his hat and went in search of

Everett. He found the manager checking over the tools in the smithy.

"Any of this stuff belong to you?" he asked Geoff.

"Nothing except that Stanner rifle in the bag on that hook. She's got my name on the bag, see? You'll find practically everything of Uncle's is either chisel-stamped or has his initials burnt on. Now I'll just shove my rifle in the car and we'll get away."

It was two hours before they returned. They found the Minton drawn up at the gate. But there seemed to be some sort of argument going on between Blue and Dogfoot. The big black was holding a day-old lamb, apparently between thumb and finger, and looking hopefully at Blue. The latter shook his head vigorously.

"You leavem that feller lamb!" he said sternly. "Mister Everett findem mother blong him quick-fellow." Dogfoot nodded sadly and set the lamb gently on the ground again.

"Wants to take this lamb along," Blue complained to Everett and Geoff. "It's the one bad habit the beggar's got, collecting mislaid children, so to speak. If I didn't put my foot down we'd have dozens of 'em on our hands."

Everett laughed heartily.

"We found this lamb's mother up the hill there, stuck in a fence. Mr. Mason says she's a professional wire eater."

"Likes to be different, too," Geoff chuckled. "Can't have her lamb in the autumn or spring, like other ewes. This little joker'll be her property, nothing surer."

All three shook hands with Everett and, with Blue at the wheel, they were away, running easily down the farm track and through the gate on to the road. As Geoff watched Blue's handling of the big car he knew he was watching a born driver. He knew, too, that Blue, despite his attempt to hide it, was fascinated by the big Minton, revelling in the power and smoothness that seemed to pour from her twelve murmuring cylinders and in the feather-light balance of her steering. Soon they were approaching the town. The road swung right at a paddock corner. It was a bad corner, its ditches a jungle of overgrown gum suckers. And, as they swung the turn Geoff tensed; for, out of the gap in the packed trees a heavy lorry was charging straight at them. There were yards only between the vehicles; a second only till the truck crashed into them. . . . Blue scarcely seemed to notice the on-coming menace, yet his hands and feet moved with the speed of light and he had changed down to second gear. The long-bodied Minton seemed literally to spring across the road. . . . And in that flash they were clear. Then Blue was looking gloomily ahead once more. Geoff grinned. He had taken this chap for a boy who could be depended upon. He hadn't been wrong. The beggar hadn't turned a hair! Smooth work! . . . Blue saw his look.

"That truck driver's about six years old," he growled. "I bet he doesn't know yet he was right across the road. But I bet he never saw a car that could jump right out of trouble like this beauty, either!"

"Neither have I," Geoff grinned. "And, if he's as scared as I was his hair won't go down till Tuesday week!"

By now they were turning into the long street that led to the hotel.

"Well," Blue said, "I suppose the next thing is, when do we start for Queensland?" Geoff nodded.

"I've been thinking, that is, as well as I could for watching your nice driving, feller. No wonder you had no trouble getting a special driver's licence. Well, what's wrong with starting to-day? What supplies we want can all be bought in Toowoomba and I can get all the work I want done on the Minton there too. We'll have all the time we want for buying our gear while she's being slicked up."

"Ha!" Blue said and nodded non-commitally, but Geoff knew well enough that he was pleased to be pushing on.

Geoff had the key of their room. The others stood behind him in the hotel corridor while he unlocked and pushed open the door. He started to enter, then stopped.

"Forget something?" Blue asked.

For answer Geoff stepped aside and waved a hand through the door, and he was smiling grimly. The beds and floor were strewn with clothes and belongings, the drawers that had held them tossed on their sides or left lying upside down.

Half an hour later the two white boys sat on Geoff's bed and three suitcases stood side by side on the floor before them. Wardrobe and dressing table drawers were back in their places and the room was straight once more. They had decided against reporting the ransacking of their belongings.

"It's not as though we don't know who did it and what they were after and we'd only be putting Jim Carter and the staff to a lot of trouble for nothing," Geoff said. "Added to which, the police might have to keep us hanging round here for quite a while."

Blue tilted his head and looked sadly at the ceiling. "Well, well," he said softly. "All that bother and those poor chaps found no map, all because you took it with you, this morning. They must love you more than ever now, feller."

Geoff grinned but, while Blue had been speaking, he had taken out his wallet and had unfolded the charred map. He laid it down on the bed.

"Now, see here, Blue, I've come to the conclusion a thing like this map is the worst possible property. To keep it safe one of us has to cart it around and even so there's always the chance of being robbed of it. But, hang it, there's little enough detail in it. What do you say we both take a good squint at it, then see if we can re-draw it from memory. If we can, the best way to put a spoke in Graster's wheel is to burn the map."

Blue looked at him in unfeigned surprise. Then a slow grin spread over his face. He bent down, reopened his suitcase and produced a writing pad. In five minutes each of them had drawn his sketch complete with names and the scrawl beneath and compared it with the original. The result convinced them that they both had an accurate mental picture of the half-charred document.

"Right!" Geoff said at last and struck a match, and presently the two were looking at a writhing little pile of paper ash on a large ash-tray. The little heap was what remained of the original map, the two copies and, to leave nothing to chance, several blank sheets from the writing pad that might have taken some impression of their drawings.

With his pencil, Blue patted the hot ashes into fine powder.

"Now, Mr. Graster," he growled. "See what you can make of that lot!"

CHAPTER EIGHT

DOGFOOT'S NIGHT OUT

IT WAS a week later. The trio were over the New South Wales border and in the South Queensland town of Toowoomba. The Minton was her beautiful self again, panels rolled out and flashing with new duco, her new windscreen sweeping back to her new, low-set hood—a thing of beauty and power. A low-slung trailer was pivoted behind her, built with an eye to the lovely lines of the car herself and ducoed to match her. Blue leant forward, one foot on the "pole" of the trailer.

"Shoving a car like that out into the back country! Doesn't seem right!" he growled. Geoff laughed.

"Well, that's where she's going," he said. "She's got a lot of honest work to do."

The shop foreman came briskly across the wide concrete floor.

"How do you like the trailer, lad?"

"You've done a job and a half," Geoff answered. "But how about those extra understruts? I'll get you to put her on the hoist for me, if you don't mind."

"Sure," the engineer said cheerfully. A minute later, the trailer uncoupled, the big sports was high in the air and Geoff and Blue were inspecting four massive steel struts set across the chassis, two protecting the engine sump, one under the gear box and the fourth beneath the differential housing.

"A good move, that," the engineer commented. "These low-slung jobs can get into serious trouble on back country roads, but those struts will take nearly any sort of a crack."

Ten minutes later Blue eased the car and her trailer through the street entrance of the hotel yard, then nosed the outfit smoothly up to the long lock-up garage Geoff had booked when they had arrived at the hotel a week ago. The latter started to get out to unlock the doors when Dogfoot spoke abruptly from the dicky seat behind him.

"Might be feller come stealem car. More better me sleep longa 'im."

Blue glanced back at the speaker, then looked at Geoff.

"Not such a bad idea at that," he said. "I don't reckon anybody would be fool enough to steal a car as easily recognised as this, but we've stored a lot of gear in this shed and plenty of people have seen us shoving it in here. It's been on my mind a bit because none of these garages would be so darned hard to break into. Might as well play safe the last night, anyhow." He turned again to the big black-fellow.

"Okay Dogfoot, we fixem bed longa car shed."

Dogfoot watched with considerable satisfaction while they set up a folding stretcher beside the big Minton. When it was done Geoff locked the garage again and they all went up to their room.

"Well now, just for that," Blue said as he sat down on his bed, "I think we could stand Dogfoot a treat to-night. You noticed that travelling carnival in town? Well, Dogfoot looks on carnivals as the modernised version of a corroboree, but a big improvement on same. How about taking a walk round to the affair after dinner, Geoff?"

"Sure," Geoff laughed.

"Good," Blue said. "Dogfoot, we catchem kai-kai then go longa merry-go-round."

The giant's grin testified his full approval. He stood up at once, picked up his soap and towel and left in search of a shower. Blue smiled faintly.

"That shows he's pretty extra keen, you know. When the old gazooker wants something specially I've known him to use up a whole cake of soap before putting his proposition."

Presently the two friends followed Dogfoot's example and showered and changed for the evening. Dinner over, they all set off along a side street to a vacant lot a travelling outfit had set up its tents on. As they approached, strident music reached them and Geoff grinned as he watched Dogfoot. The big blackfellow threw up his head, lengthened his stride and led the way. They caught up with him in the glare of lights from a kind of revolving platform fitted with chairs. The platform spun like a gramophone disc carrying the chairs round with it. But, in addition, each chair spun on its own pivot, one way then the other, as fancy took it. They seemed to like their job, those chairs, and they got worked up about it and fairly whizzed clockwise, then anti-clockwise. Geoff and Blue regarded the entire works with suspicion and either would have preferred the worst storm at sea. To Dogfoot, however, the machine seemed an old friend. He accepted the two tickets Blue Campbell bought him and took a chair. The machine started and as the chair, after a few preliminary whizzes, settled down to business, his grin reached for his ears.

A man behind them was bawling details of the benefits to be derived from a visit to his spear-throwing gallery. Hit the bull's-eye once and you collected many cigarettes. Hit it three times and the wealth you would amass would make King Solomon blink. There were even electric jugs, alarm clocks, sets of cutlery and cut glass of such rarity as only Indian rajahs could possibly afford. Geoff saw that Blue was eyeing the spruiker with a sort of grim speculation and when Dogfoot, having just finished an anti-clockwise whizzing that seemed to make a complete circle of his grin, ended his second ride in stately, slow clockwise motion, Blue beckoned him over. With a jerk of his head he indicated the spruiker now holding up an alarm clock that glittered temptingly in the glare from his stall. Already there was a small crowd before the booth. Dogfoot looked over their heads. It is doubtful if he understood a word of the harangue, but the three spears in the man's hand and that shining clock held aloft told him all he wanted to know. He stepped at once to the tiny box office, completely filled by a tiny woman who was evidently the spruiker's staff, and pushed in six shillings. The woman laughed and pushed out six tickets. Dogfoot solemnly packed five into the pocket of his shirt, then walked across and handed one to the spruiker.

Already a man was throwing at the target but

he seemed to be having trouble with the wommera, or throwing stick, the spruiker had provided. His first spear was sticking in the sawdust before the target. Then he abandoned the wommera, took the spear shaft in his hand and threw it. It merely skidded along the wall of the canvas gallery, turned a somersault and dropped ignominiously on the sawdust. The crowd chuckled good-naturedly and the spruiker spoke encouragingly.

"A bit higher, next time, matey. Try again, now." Then he was bawling again. "Don't forget, ladies and gentlemen there's a wide choice o' prizes. A wonderful chance to combine fun and profit. The spears is made for me special by the best spear-maker on the Alligator River. Get your tickets at the window. Aw, that's better matey! A bit more practice and you'll be set for the big winnin's!"

His customer's last throw had found the edge of the target but the spear had jumped off and fallen to the ground. Two more throwers were ahead of Dogfoot. Both managed to set a spear in the target but a long way from its centre. The spruiker's condolences belied the satisfaction in his eyes.

"Better luck next time, matey," he bawled to the last thrower. "Plenty o' prizes, ladies and gentlemen, all sent to me special from me overseas connections. Hit the bull's-eye and take your choice. Get your tickets—Okay, big boy, you're next."

Geoff thought he looked a trifle uneasy as Dogfoot stepped up and a few passers-by, seeing the big blackfellow with a handful of spears, joined the little crowd. Dogfoot didn't keep them waiting. The wommera seemed to fit itself to the shaft end, a long arm came back, there was a flash and a thud—then a great shout from the crowd. The spear was stuck, quivering, in the black bull's-eye in the target's centre. But almost at once Dogfoot threw again. A second spear thudded into the black centre. And then the crowd roared; for the third spear flashed the length of the gallery and somehow wedged itself right between the other two.

Every man in the crowd was shouting and several slapped the big blackfellow on the back. People came streaming to the booth from all round. Such a press at his gallery should have delighted the spruiker. Instead, however, he was scowling. But neither his scowl nor the back-slapping of the crowd seemed to have any effect upon Dogfoot. The giant was pointing calmly at an alarm clock.

"Feller sing out longa stomach ache," he said quietly to the spruiker. The crowd shouted again with delight. With a forced smile the spruiker reached and handed over the clock.

"There you are, me lad. Nobody has ever been able to say Jim Corney didn't deliver the goods. You made three of the best throws I ever seen. Get your tickets, ladies and gentlemen."

Dogfoot took the clock and placed it carefully on a little ledge of the stall beside him. Then he reached in his pocket, drew out another ticket and handed it, without comment, to the spruiker. The geniality vanished once more from that worthy's face but the crowd was more delighted than ever.

"Go on, sport, give him another bundle. Give him a fair go!"

The spruiker was cornered and he knew it. Somehow he worked up a grin and handed over the spears. Shouts came from all round.

"Do it again, Goliath! Show him it wasn't a fluke!" Still Dogfoot didn't seem even aware that he was the centre of attraction. His lithe body leaned a little sideways, his throwing arm just clear of his body. Geoff watched him closely. But what followed was too fast for the eye. All Geoff and the crowd knew was that three spears seemed actually in the air together. Then all three were bunched, quivering, in the bull's-eye of the target.

The crowd's roar brought every person not yet before the spear gallery hurrying to it. Men were once again clapping Dogfoot on the back. The giant's only movement, now, however, was to raise his pointing finger, pointing inexorably at another alarm clock, with which the spruiker's staff had replaced the first one; a bright red one this time, squat built, with a double bell. Amid shouts of "Come on, sport, he wants the big red clock," the spruiker bent and lifted it. The black's vast hand clamped around it and set it beside the other. But when the hand slid again into his shirt pocket for one more ticket the laughter was deafening.

Blue and Geoff had stood all the time within a yard of Dogfoot and Blue was watching the spruiker closely. Now, as Dogfoot calmly proffered his third ticket Blue caught the spruiker's eye and his head jerked almost imperceptibly. The other looked at him hard, hesitated, then, for the third time he forced a grin, strode down the canvas alleyway, drew out the spears and handed them to Dogfoot. That done he slipped out to Blue and Geoff, waiting in the shadow behind his booth. Blue wasted no time.

"It's like this," he said. "This big joker is my responsibility. You've got to make a living and you don't bargain for customers like him. As a matter of fact you don't know yet what you're up against. If you'd seen him do the things with spears that I have, you'd know hitting that bull's-eye in there at this distance is like eating porridge to him. Now look, here's ten pounds. Let him keep throwing till you reckon he's won a few more prizes and there's a fair profit left for you. Then give me the nod and I'll take him away."

Out of the glare of the booth lights there was something likeable about the spruiker's face. In fact it was just the face of a family man, and pretty well lined with worry. It seemed to take him several seconds to grasp what Blue had said. Then, the ten pound note in his hand, he was grinning, but his grin was a little shame-faced.

"Why—why hang it, that's fair enough. In fact, it's a darned sight better than fair, young feller. I'll admit I'm a bit worried to-night. Had some poor runs and all that stuff ain't paid for yet. And when that Man Friday o' yours—My gosh, there he goes again!" There came another quick series of thuds and another concerted yell from the crowd. When they reached the front once more Dogfoot's finger was pointing at yet another alarm clock, this time a small one, mottled green and yellow. The spruiker picked it up and now there was no scowl on his face. The crowd laughed when he twiddled the hands and the little clock gave forth a shrill peal.

"Take a look at him, ladies and gentlemen," he bawled. "You're seeing an exhibition o' skill you're never likely to see again. It seems he likes plenty of alarm clocks around him. Well, that's all right with Jim Corney." He had shut off the alarm and now handed the clock with a flourish to Dogfoot. Cries of "Good man! Fair enough!" came from the crowd as the giant set his latest clock down with the others.

It was half an hour later that the trio paused on a street corner a block away from the carnival. Dogfoot was wearing a broad belt studded with plated, shining rivets. He held two alarm clocks in one hand and the big red one strung on a finger of the other, which also held several safety razors in shining cases. A large umbrella hung over his left arm. His shirt pockets and the pockets of his shorts bulged with packets of cigarettes. Under his right arm was a large tin dish and from the hip pocket of his badly strained shorts protruded a daintily coloured box of toilet soap. An offer by Geoff to carry some of his wealth was politely but firmly refused. The street light glinted on his tin dish and flashed on his wide grin. Geoff suppressed his own grin as they moved on again.

"A chap who's as good with spears as that ought to be a darned good rifle shot," he said to Blue. But Blue shook his head.

"I thought so too. But it seems that, when the old gazooker was a kid a chap gave him an old rifle that was badly leaded.* The first time Dogfoot fired it it exploded and he had a bad headache for a fortnight. Since then he hasn't had a lot of time for guns."

An hour later still Blue and Geoff sat yarning on the hotel balcony. Dogfoot had gone to bed in the garage. Suddenly the quiet of the hotel yard below them was shattered by metallic pandemonium. It was the bell of an alarm clock. But scarcely had it got well started when there came a second urgent clamour an octave higher, a shrill soprano skirling. For a full minute the soprano shrilled and the tenor hammered hard. Then, to their joint effort was suddenly added a racketing so diabolic that Geoff started up. It filled the wide yard with a noise like a bass-voiced tom-cat trailing tin cans and cursing as he went. It brought startled heads to windows. Blue chuckled.

"I showed him how to set 'em all for nine o'clock," he said. "But that last one's standing in his tin dish. I told him if he put it there it'd sing out longa ten stomach ache."

*Not "loaded." A badly fouled rifle will shred lead from bullets till at last a bullet will lodge in the barrel. If the rifle is a cheap one the result will be a split breach and a serious concussion to the shooter.

CHAPTER NINE

THE AMBUSH

TWO BOYS clad in shorts and shirts sat either side of a little camp fire whose fluttering blaze paled with the broadening light of dawn. Both were looking at a dead tree standing alone in the wide flatness, its branches like skeleton arms pointing jagged bone ends at the fiery east. Blue Campbell spoke gloomily:

"One saltbush plain inhabited by one dead tree!"

Geoff chuckled.

"Well, we've come a long way to see it, Blue. You've put 783 miles on the speedo since we left Toowoomba. What's more we've got quite a way to go yet. We cross Spinifex Creek about seventy miles from here by the map. Then the thing the map calls a road swings north to Burramoola."

He came to his feet with the lithe ease of an athelete and looked again across the plain to the east. "If Graster and his gangsters are still on our trail they've used up some petrol, that's one thing. Anyhow, they're not camping where we can see them, but I don't suppose they think they're called upon to do that."

Blue tilted his head and squinted at the dawn sky:

"Speaking of trails, there's that car ahead of us—

we seem to be catching up on it." He got up. "Well, here comes Dogfoot."

Geoff shook his head.

"Mystery man, that feller," he grinned. "We'd no sooner got into the flat country than he dispenses with boots. Now he just gets up from breakfast and jogs off on a five mile circle of the camp. What's his idea?"

Blue chuckled. "As for boots, he's worn boots for two years. But the soles of his feet are still half an inch thick. And as for his strolling off, you've got to remember that joker's pretty near out in his own country here. From now on you'll find he'll be able to tell us every morning whether anything on two legs or four has been within a couple of miles of the camp during the night."

The giant came towards them at a long lope as they set about collecting camp gear and packing it in the trailer. Within speaking distance, however, he dropped to a walk and strode forward. Blue straightened from rolling a blanket, looked at him hard and suddenly groaned loudly.

"I might have known!"

"Hullo, what's wrong?" Geoff asked in surprise.

For answer Blue continued to scowl at the approaching black. Dogfoot held something in his left hand. He stopped before them and held it out. It was a tiny wallaby, some eight inches or so long, covered in pearly grey fur and with wide eyes that surveyed them steadily. Dogfoot stood still and wordless, cupping the little fellow in his great hand. But the eyes that looked out of his bearded face at Blue were full of a child-like anxiety.

"Now, here we go again!" Blue lamented. "I thought it was too good to be true, coming 783 miles without this feller collecting a motherless something. Dogfoot, where you findem piccaninny wallaby?"

The answer came promptly.

"Dingo bin chasem mudder belong 'im. Dingo come up close mudder belong 'im. Mudder belong 'im peltem 'im into tanna bush." As he spoke Dogfoot gave an astonishingly accurate pantomime of a wallaby plucking her joey from her pouch. ". . . mudder belong 'im foolem dingo. Mudder belong 'im. . . ."

"Oh, for heck's sake, all right, all right!" Blue cried. He turned to Geoff. "I told you the old gazooker would pick up every darned track round the camp. But apparently all he's found is the tracks of a dingo pack hard-pressing a wallaby. He's found where she threw out her joey and wheeled to draw the pack away. The chances are ten to one the dogs pulled her down before daylight. They never let up, those jokers. But the point is, Dogfoot's brought in the joey and you can see for yourself how he feels about the little blighter." Leaning on the left door of the Minton Geoff's amused glance moved from the disgusted speaker to the eager face of the big hunter. When he spoke his voice was shaking with suppressed laughter.

"Okay with me, feller," he said. "Let's see what he can do."

Blue sighed, reached grimly into a corner of the trailer and drew out a tin of condensed milk. Without speaking he handed it to Dogfoot. At once the anxiety in the black's face gave way to a flashing grin. He took the milk, laid the joey on the ground, whipped out his knife and punctured the tin. Within a minute, to Geoff's further amusement, he had mixed some milk in a pannikin. Then he produced a piece of string from somewhere, dipped it in the milk and held its dripping end over the joey's nose. Immediately the wide-eyed youngster turned a somersault in Dogfoot's vast hand and waited for the dripping string to be lowered into his mouth for all joeys drink upside down. Between dips, the joey looked up at Dogfoot with growing admiration. His whole attitude seemed to say that things might be tough but here was one chap a fellow could rely on. Looking at the bearded black on his knees with that tiny ball of grey fur in one hand, it seemed to Geoff he had never seen two so thoroughly satisfied people. Blue sighed again, tossed the last of the bundles to his friend, stamped out the fire and sprinkled it with water, while Geoff, laughing quietly, set about buttoning down the trailer's canvas cover.

Within half an hour, and as the sun's rim flung level light shafts across the plain, the Minton moved away. Dogfoot and the joey shared the dicky seat. The little fellow leaned back, propped in his corner and regarded his benefactor steadily and with complete approval. The road led away north-west, twisting just enough to lose itself in the short salt bush so that it seemed always about to fade out altogether half a mile ahead. Indeed it was now no more than a track. So far as they could gather, it was used mainly by a small mail truck that made the trip once a week. For an hour the Minton droned across the grey, green carpet. Here and there in loose patches in the road the tyre marks of a well-shod car showed clearly.

Blue turned back to Dogfoot.

"How long that feller car bin makem track?"

As always with Dogfoot, the answer came promptly. "Makem yestiddy close up sun 'im sleep."

Blue nodded. "Couldn't have been much ahead of us when we pulled up to camp at sundown yesterday," he said to Geoff.

Presently, far ahead, they saw a whitish blob that seemed actually to dance on the horizon.

"That'll be Duny, I reckon," Geoff said. "The chap back at Muntera said we can fill up with petrol there and save drawing on our spare drum."

"That must be the pub," Blue grinned, half an hour later, as they drove down what was not so much a street as just a dusty space between a dozen houses. He pointed to a wooden cottage leaning crazily eastward and apparently ready to collapse on its occupants (if any) the very next time the wind blew from the west. "Glad we didn't bother coming on this far last night. Rather camp out any time than try to sleep in a hen house like that."

It would almost seem that the joey heard his remark for he stretched his neck and looked over the door. And apparently he agreed with Blue entirely for he wriggled back into his corner and returned at once to his admiration of Dogfoot. Three men squatted on their heels under a pepper tree near the hotel's corner and looked hard at the big sports car as she purred past. Blue drew to a standstill before a faded red bowser that was the one touch of colour in the paintless front of a wooden store. A lean, sandy-complexioned man strolled out to them. After an exchange of greetings he told them his name was Wilkes and began to pump the bowser; but his chief interest seemed to be the Minton and her trailer. When, presently, he paused to let the petrol he had pumped rumble into her tank he stood back and looked the outfit over from end to end. The Minton's length and rakish lines and the long sleek bonnet seemed to fascinate Mr. Wilkes more and more the longer he looked.

Finally he shook his head.

"I never saw a car like this only in pictures," he volunteered. "Must've set you back a few quid, a car like that. The only . . ." Clearly, he was about to tell them something that had interested him but at that moment the trailer caught his eye again.

"Gee," he exclaimed. He stepped from the bowser and laid a hairy hand on the side of the trailer. Next instant he had sprung back as though shot. For, from under the canvas cover, came a sudden, clamorous whirring. The man's protruding eyes stayed fixed on the finger-marks his hand had left on the trailer's dust-coated surface, as though he expected a rattlesnake's head to dart through. But the effect on Dogfoot was quite the opposite. He just sat and grinned. It was clear the appalling racket was music in his ears. Blue turned and eyed him grimly, then looked gloomily at Geoff who was choking back his laughter. Finally he spoke to the astonished storekeeper.

"You pressed the right spot the first time, Mr. Wilkes!"

"Brrrrrrrrrrrrrr!"

This time it was the metallic baritone of the big red clock and it thundered out from the opposite corner of the trailer. The hammering of both clocks together brought a look of such utter bliss to Dogfoot and such consternation to Mr. Wilkes that Geoff could hold back his spluttering no longer. Blue was on the point of addressing Mr. Wilkes once more but that gentleman's sandy complexion had turned to dirty cream and already he had backed into his store entrance. Clearly, he wanted no further dealings with an outfit that whirred when you touched it. He stood and watched while Dogfoot climbed out and helped Geoff fill the water bags, replenish the drums and check the radiator. Even then he came no more than two steps to take payment for the petrol and reached hurriedly into his trousers pocket for change. True, he went so far as to mention that it was 188 miles to Delaney and that the road was plain and dry but that an early storm had started Spinifex Creek running. Having told them that, he wheeled and stalked inside.

"Didn't invite us in," Geoff grinned as Blue let in the clutch and they drove away.

"We'll have to take a couple of those confounded clocks away from Dogfoot, that's all about it," Blue grumbled. "The things'll have us tabbed for lunatics from one side of Queensland to the other.

In three towns they frightened three different old ladies—scared 'em badly; in Norton they made a horse bolt and in Cornell they woke up those confounded twin babies. Was that a show!"

Geoff nodded and choked again.

"I'll say!" he said when he could speak. "If it hadn't been for the two nippers finally taking a fancy to Dogfoot himself we all might have finished up in clink. But it's your own fault, you darned old fraud, from start to finish. In the first place you gave him all the help you could to win those clocks. Then you went to a lot of trouble showing him how to manage them. He shuts 'em off at night, as instructed but he looks forward to having them do their stuff during the day. You can't go and spoil his fun now."

"If you only knew when to *expect* 'em!" Blue growled again, "or whether one'll go off or the whole confounded battery!—For heck's sake, now what do *you* want?"

The last remark was to the joey. Neither the purr of the Minton's twelve cylinders nor the whirring of Dogfoot's clocks seemed to have upset that small marsupial but apparently he had reached the conclusion that there was a whole lot in the world he hadn't known about and he'd better take a look. He found footing on Dogfoot's knees and peered through the windscreen between Geoff and Blue, his long ears standing straight out from his head. Obviously, if there was astonishment about, he was ready for it. Geoff chuckled again but next moment he was pointing at a bulge on the horizon ahead.

"That'll be the timbered ridge this side of Spinifex Creek. How about a spot of kai there, feller?"

Blue nodded.

"Should find a spot of shade there. I see the tracks of that car are still ahead of us. If that storekeeper hadn't lost his nerve he'd have told us all about them."

The distant ridge was twenty miles away but the smooth speed of the long-bodied sports car brought it rapidly into clear view. Presently they were looking at a chain of rocky hills timbered with a ragged spread of black wattle and a kind of woolly-butt with rough black bark and gnarled branches. The saltbush gave way at last to a wide patch of spinifex grass and then to tufted ridge grass. The narrow track swung left along the ridge foot for half a mile, and they soon knew why; for when it turned sharply to the right again, they saw that it led straight into a narrow gorge. Blue let the speedo drop back to fifteen miles an hour as the big car faced the rocky climb, finally drawing to a standstill in the shade of a woolly-butt on the left of the track.

"How about this one?"

"Fine," Geoff answered. They all got out and Dogfoot, putting the joey on the ground, set quietly but swiftly about making a fire. Geoff stood still, looking up where the road ahead snaked through the narrow gorge. Rocks claim the attention of any one interested in boring for water or in mining. But it was the gorge itself, rather than the rocks that formed it that held his gaze now. He studied it for several minutes while Blue and Dogfoot lifted out the tucker box from the trailer. At last he spoke.

"I reckon I'll take a stroll along this ridge, if you fellers have no objection to doing all the work while I'm away."

"Sure. And we'll have the fire burning nice and bright to warm you when you get back. But, hang it, son, what's wrong with a drink of tea and a meal first, in this shade? It's hot enough up amongst those boulders to fry eggs, I bet."

Geoff laughed. "I'll be back by the time the billy boils. I'll take my hardware, though. Might knock over one of those rabbits they say have migrated out here."

"A rock wallaby, more likely. Only for Pete's sake don't fetch back anything motherless."

Geoff slipped his rifle from its straps under the canvas of the trailer and drew it from its bag. It was the Stanner he had brought from the farm, a high velocity rifle that whipped away a bullet with venomous speed. He checked the magazine, thrust a handful of the big, bottle shaped shells in a pocket of his shorts and then set off.

Ten minutes clambering brought him to a dolomite boulder half-way up the ridge and about a quarter of a mile away to the right from the car. He climbed round it and turned left up the steep slope. He worked still more to the left, till he was climbing the ridge obliquely and actually heading back towards the gorge. His eyes flickered right and left as he moved and he chose his footing carefully. The heat amongst the rocks was fierce, as Blue had predicted, and perspiration poured from his face and neck; but he held on steadily, making no sound.

Close to the crest at last, the boy dropped to a

crouch, looked quickly to right and left again, then faced straight up the slope. Ten seconds later he was easing his body forward on hands and knees between two small boulders. From there he could see over the razor-back as well as along the ridge to the lip of the gorge, but the car behind him on his left was hidden by the strewn boulders of the hill-side. The two rocks between which he lay had already had six hours of summer sun. The heat they flung out at him almost seared the skin of his face and arms and bare legs, and the pebbly surface he lay on was actually burning both legs and arms. Then, in a flash, he forgot the burning ground and stifling air.

He had found what he had come to look for.

A hundred yards down the farther slope, half in the black shadow of a three-foot boulder, a man lay with a rifle by his side, half his faded red shirt turned grey by the rock's shadow. Fifty yards beyond him and somewhat closer to the gorge, was another man, a thick-set man with a black hat pulled over his eyes. He sat on the ground, his back to a rock, knees bent and a rifle in his lap.

Geoff's mouth set hard. The man's face was in shadow but there was no mistaking those heavy shoulders and the bull neck. This was the man who had tried to shoot him down as he ran from the ruins of the farmhouse, the man Dirk!

It was clear enough why the two were there. From where they waited they could see down the rock-strewn slope into the farther end of the gorge. A car climbing slowly up that narrow way would be within point-blank range for perhaps a hundred

hoarse shout joined the echoes from the roaring Stanner. He fell heavily on his right shoulder, regained his feet and, half screaming, half shouting, went plunging down the slope towards his companion. Both his hands were outstretched before him and his eyes bulged from his blood-smeared face. To the other man he must have looked a badly wounded man, and it was clear he had no rifle. Blackhat had drawn an automatic from a shoulder holster but he knew well this man with the high velocity rifle had him hopelessly outranged, and if he had any thought of waiting to help his henchman, it vanished when a snarling bullet seemed actually to nick his left ear. He wheeled and plunged down among the boulders ahead of his half-blinded accomplice. He sprang sideways from a bullet that spattered on a boulder beside his left knee, then back again from one that splashed on a vertical outcrop two inches from his head. And to Redshirt, floundering behind him, it seemed that whatever he touched shed a bullet. He snatched back his hand from a slab of granite that gave forth a vicious whine right under his reaching fingers, fell headlong again, sprang up and plunged on. But in ten more strides he had plunged over into the gorge after his companion.

Geoff was on his feet now. His rifle's magazine was empty at last but he was ready to load and fire single shots if need be. Already, however, his enemies were out of sight. He swiftly re-filled the magazine, then set off at a run along the slope. But, before he reached the edge of the gorge he heard the roar of a light engine and the scream of gears. Then he saw the car, a kind of converted utility, hurtling down the track. Already it had left the gorge and was lurching madly out on to the plain. Next moment it had swung off the road to the right and, still rocking to the urge of wide open throttle, shot away north-eastward across the saltbush, heading up along the left bank of Spinifex Creek.

The lad halted, panting, and watched it go, a white wisp of smoke still curling from his rifle muzzle. Hmph! These killers liked shooting all right so long as they were doing it! Well, these two would be a bit more respectful in future!

He heard a shout from behind him and Dogfoot came running over the razor-back, Blue a hundred yards back. He watched the giant springing down to him through the boulders with the swiftness of a hunter born. Was this the man who had ridden on a razzle-dazzle among a score of small children?

"Okay, Dogfoot," he said when the black halted beside him, his chest scarcely heaving from the gruelling run. "Me bin scarem bad-one white feller."

Blue had dropped to a walk when he saw Geoff speak to Dogfoot. He carried the shotgun and his pockets bulged with shells.

Ten minutes later the trio stood on the plain looking down at where dual car tracks turned off the road north-eastward.

"Must be camped up the creek somewhere," Blue commented. "And, boy, were they in a hurry to get back to their camp!" He held up the shot gun. "Wish I'd got one pot at 'em after all. Over five yards I'm a bit inaccurate. Too highly strung, I suppose! But, feller, did you set up a hullabaloo amongst those rocks! I couldn't tell echoes from shots in the end and I thought you'd been set upon by a big bunch of fellers. But I reckon those two birds must've thought you had a machine-gun in each hand!"

CHAPTER TEN

THE CROSSING

THE SUN, still overhead, beat into the low hood of the Minton as she swept across the plain.

"Ye gods, it's hot now, all right," Geoff grinned. "Well, there's the creek right ahead, anyhow. If there's not enough water still in it for a swim I'll be annoyed with the thing."

Within half a mile the road led round a long, narrow neck of scrub and next moment they caught the gleam of water.

"Good!" Geoff exclaimed. "Why, hallo! . . . Suffering Caesar!"

Right before them now, the road led into rippling shallows, the water of a wide creek flowing over gravel. But the boy's last exclamations came not from that but from the sight of a car out in the middle of the glittering stream. It was a big sedan, a green Packard, and it had got off to the left side of the gravel bar that formed the crossing for the road. In trying to get back to the road bed its driver had swung it facing directly upstream; but he had failed to get it back and judging by the car's tilt from front to back, the rear wheels were deep in a hole. Then, as Blue let the Minton coast down the gentle slope to within ten yards of the water's edge, a man appeared from the opposite side of the bogged sedan. Geoff, his eyes on the sedan, sat forward with a jerk.

"Good heavens! . . . Great Cæsar, it can't be!"

Blue cut the engine, then turned an unsmiling face to his friend.

"Now, what would this babbling be about? I remarked when we left the gorge that there was still a car ahead of us and you said yes there was. Now I see a car bogged in a creek. Also, I see a man standing in the water beside it. But I see nothing to babble about."

But Geoff didn't seem to hear him. His eyes were fixed on the man who had waded round in front of the sedan, a fat man with a bristling grey moustache and a light bandage round his neck. Shirt and shorts were no disguise. That round body, that moustache and that bandaged neck were all stamped on his memory. . . . It was Monsieur Montserrat!

But Monsieur, too, was gazing spellbound. Clearly he was in sore need of help and a car was what he wanted most. But even such a happy surprise did not account for his reaction. He gazed a moment longer, then suddenly he was charging towards them, the spray of his charge flying high about him. Blue said afterwards he looked like a panicked hippo some of the time and a bolting paddle-steamer the rest of it. However that may be, Monsieur seemed to gather speed as he came and by the time Geoff had scrambled out of the Minton, he leapt ashore and came up the short slope at a sort of waddling gallop, water pouring from his legs and sandals into the dust of the road.

"M'sieur Geoff! M'sieur Geoff! *Le bon Dieu*!

Marie! *Voilà*! Look what we see *ma chère*! God is good! M'sieur Geoff is 'ere!"

But in spite of his astonishment and delight Geoff was not to be taken unawares again and have himself hugged to Monsieur's bosom. He held out his hand.

"Great Cæsar, M'sieur, what the deuce are you doing over this side of Queensland? Why. . . ."

But the old man had grasped his hand and was talking less English and more French every moment. Geoff flung a quick side glance at Blue and was relieved to see that his friend was quite equal to the situation. Blue's poker face registered only polite interest in Monsieur's high-speed gesticulation and higher speed French.

But it was soon clear to Geoff that Monsieur's oratory was getting them nowhere at all. One thing, of course, needed no explanation. There was Monsieur's car in the creek, a Packard with her radiator pointing at the brazen sky; and, in the car, was poor Madame, once more a prisoner. And now, as though to make mention of this fact, Madame somehow squeezed herself past the steering wheel and pushed open the driver's door. She was none the less a prisoner, however, for all round her the creek water rippled and flashed in the sunlight, and though Madame had seen much of the world, about Western Queensland creeks she had, as yet, formed no definite opinions. True, she had seen Monsieur get safely ashore in a cloud of spray but also she had seen the car sink deep into the creek bottom. In short, she wasn't prepared to wade ashore. And the obvious alternative was to carry her out.

When one finds a lady surrounded by water it seems a simple duty to carry her to safety. Geoff's trouble, however, was that Madame was no ordinary damsel in distress. He didn't know her weight but he did know he couldn't carry her. He even doubted if he and Blue together could do it, even provided they could devise some means of securing a reliable grip upon Madame. The unbroken stream of French still pouring from Monsieur didn't help him to think clearly.

To tow the car out with Madame in it seemed the only way but she'd be scared of the thing capsizing. He turned a despairing face to Blue.

"It's easy," Blue said solemnly. He stepped out of the Minton and spoke to Dogfoot.

"You catchem white feller missus longa creek. Quickfellow!"

The suggestion didn't seem to surprise Dogfoot any more than if he had been asked to pass the salt. He turned and strode into the water. His movement brought an exclamation of delight from Monsieur. Here, apparently, was one who understood him perfectly! He wheeled and splashed into the stream beside Dogfoot. Geoff followed, his despairing frown already replaced by a grin.

When they reached the car Madame forgot her peril entirely in the joy of greeting him. She held his hand in both of hers, then released him to use them for exclaiming with. She exclaimed and explained, laughed and pouted and laughed again. Then, at last she turned to Dogfoot. Apparently she knew well what he was there for.

And it would seem that this was not the first time

Dogfoot had carried ladies out of creeks. He bent a little and when he straightened he held Madame securely in his great arms. Then he turned and waded easily away from the car. Ten seconds later he had set her down gently on the dry road.

In the tilt of her head as she looked up at him there was something of a grace that seemed to have defied the years and her stoutness, and she was laughing gaily as she turned to Monsieur and Geoff, squattering out of the water behind her. Then she turned back, still laughing, and addressed Dogfoot.

"*Merci*, *mon ami*. I think never again to be carried! You have the strength of a lion! And, I assure you, you had need of it!"

Dogfoot understood nothing whatever of the speech but he read genuine thanks in her laughing eyes. His fine teeth flashed in a smile. Blue came up behind him, then, and introductions followed. But when they were made Geoff cut in sternly.

"Now, look here, M'sieur, before we ask any more questions, have you and Madame had lunch?"

"*Non*, *non*!" M'sieur replied, ruefully. "We would make ze repast when we 'ave cross ze rivaire. But, *diable*, instead we are in ze 'ole!"

Geoff managed to keep his voice steady as he continued. "Well, M'sieur, Dogfoot'll shove the billy on right away and Blue and I will see about your car." He pulled a ground sheet out of the trailer and spread it in the shade of a river gum. Madame sank down on it with a grateful smile but Monsieur made ready to return to his bogged sedan.

"We won't want you, M'sieur," Geoff laughed. "Sit down and watch us do our stuff."

Still the old man demurred but clearly he was almost exhausted and finally he sat down beside Madame and drew a cigar case from his shirt pocket. Blue uncoupled the trailer while Geoff went ahead with a rope. Then, with Geoff at the wheel and the Minton towing her, the big Packard came up easily out of the hole and was once more on the creek bank. Geoff untied the rope and rolled it up and then turned the Packard to face the crossing again.

He and Blue found Madame in raptures over the joey Dogfoot had brought from the Minton and was now feeding. In the end Dogfoot stood back and grinned while Madame fed the joey with a corner of her handkerchief dipped in milk. As for the joey, he looked round cheerfully between mouthfuls. Obviously, so far as he was concerned, the more fuss the better.

While they lunched and drank tea they heard Monsieur's story. When Geoff had come to their aid near Murundy the old Frenchman and Madame had been to Sydney and were then on their way back to Queensland to spend a long-promised holiday with an old friend of Monsieur's, one Dick Thornleigh, whom he had known in the Somme trenches in 1916. They had returned home to Brisbane from Murundy. Then, Monsieur's neck continuing to improve, they had set out once more, this time in Monsieur's well-tried Packard. Apparently they had no real idea of the back country in summer in spite of Mr. Thornleigh's warning letters. Geoff concluded, as the old man talked, that Madame had had an anxious week; yet, far from complaining, she added vivacious comment to Monsieur's narrative and watched him with pride and affection. According to Blue's count, however, Monsieur had got lost eighteen times and ditched his big sedan twelve times. The car's weight and her Packard engine had saved him from serious accident. Indeed, it would seem that Monsieur was long used to his car saving him from serious accident and he expected it of her. But being dropped into a deep silt hole in the middle of a flowing creek was more than even a Packard could cope with and all Monsieur's efforts to get her out had only made the rear wheels dig themselves a deeper hole.

"I am surprise!" Monsieur lamented in conclusion, looking reproachfully at the big car, her wheels now drying in the hot sun. "Nevaire before 'ave 'e be'ave so!"

But almost in the same breath he was cheerful again. He smiled eagerly at Blue and then at Geoff.

"Did not the *bon Dieu* send you again, M'sieur, Geoff. It is the chance impossible, yet you are here and, with you, M'sieur Blue and ze good Dogfoot!"

Geoff told them simply of his uncle's death and that Blue and he were following up some information that might mean a lot to them.

"And it looks as though we travel together as far as Cantilla, M'sieur. Now, you've had a gruelling morning. How about using me for a chauffeur that far? We'll wait here till the worst of the heat's done, then push on, have tea on the road at sundown and get to Cantilla fairly soon after dark."

He glanced at Madame as he spoke and saw a

flash of eager relief in her face, but it was gone in an instant and she made no comment till Monsieur had accepted the offer with enthusiasm. Then she turned to Blue.

"Ah, then, I am the back-seat driver an 'ave it all myself," she laughed. But Blue grinned and pointed to the joey, now gazing admiringly at her laughing face from a corner of the ground sheet.

"That fellow thinks you're nearly as nice as Dogfoot. You can tell by the way his ears stick out."

Madame reached and snatched him up.

"Ah, then the good Dogfoot will perhaps lend him to me," she cried. "Ah, but it is *l'enfant pathétique*, is it not?"

It was still only a little after two o'clock, the hottest hour of the day. They talked for some time longer, during which Monsieur mislaid his cigar and set fire to the ground sheet.

"Now how about a swim?" Geoff suggested. "Looks a decent place up above that mulga clump."

"*Bon*!" Madame exclaimed with a degree of enthusiasm that startled Geoff for, to tell the truth, Madame hadn't been included in his idea at all. But Madame, it seemed, had been envying the wet sandals of her escort. As for her own feet they were so 'ot it could not be believed. She meant to soak them while the menfolk were swimming.

An hour later, the four cooled by their swim and Madame by well-soaked feet, and all refreshed by more tea, they got away again, Madame and the joey in the back-seat of the Packard, Dogfoot, wearing his widest grin, seated proudly beside Blue in the Minton. Blue led the way and both cars made the crossing without mishap. The air in their faces had a suggestion of coolness now and grew gradually cooler as they drove. The road, however, had developed unexpected pot-holes, filled with dust, and Blue had to keep the pace down for fear of broken springs. In the first hour they had travelled thirty of the hundred miles between the crossing and Cantilla. Then they crossed a "pebble bar" five miles wide that slowed them to almost walking pace; after that they picked up speed once more and the long road slipped away steadily behind them.

"There's half the distance done, M'sieur," Geoff said, leaning to tap the speedometer dial. "Another fifty miles will see us in your friends' home town."

"*Non*," Monsieur objected. "It is at Cantilla that they meet us, but it is not, what you say, their 'ome town, *non*. But what is that ahead? It is ze automobile, surely. Look, Marie, *ma chère*! In two 'undred kilometre we meet but one auto! Except for M'sieur Geoff we yet would be in ze 'ole, *mais oui*!"

Again Geoff managed to smother his laughter and fixed his attention on the oncoming car winding swiftly across the wide plain. Soon it could be identified as a dusty red sedan. Then, right ahead, it began to slow down and they saw it was driven by a tall man, clean-shaven, who was looking at them keenly. A teenage girl with a mop of fair hair sat beside him.

Geoff had kept two hundred yards behind the Minton to avoid her dust. He drew up closer now for Blue swung the big sports out beside the road. But the approaching car also swung off and obviously the driver raised his hand to indicate he was stopping. Indeed it is common practice in the back country to stop before passing, for meetings are few and many miles of lonely track might lie ahead, about which it is well to ask. Geoff slowed to draw up behind the Minton and all three cars came to a standstill within a few yards of each other.

"How do!" Blue said quietly and raised his hat. The stranger responded and the girl bowed and smiled. Geoff had opened his door and stepped to the ground when a yelp from Monsieur made him jump and a shrill burst of French came from the back seat. He turned quickly to find Madame grappling with the door and he reached and opened it for her. At the same moment the Packard listed violently to starboard for it had been relieved of the vast weight of Monsieur. The old Frenchman was out and charging round in front.

"Deeck! Deeck!"

But now the man and girl, both laughing, were out of their car and they met Monsieur Montserrat half-way; or, perhaps it would be better to say that Monsieur charged into their midst and all but mowed them down. Blue said afterwards a hippopotamus charge works on the same principle. The old man hugged the tall man with one arm and the laughing girl with the other, then he was dragging them across to Madame, leaning from the Packard's open door.

It was easy to guess that the man was Dick Thornleigh, Monsieur's friend, and by this time

Geoff knew well what to expect. A vast amount of broken English and much undiluted French were required when Madame and Monsieur met their friends. He strolled forward to Blue. That worthy sat twisted at the wheel.

"Better come in out of the storm, feller," he said gloomily.

Evidently Dick Thornleigh knew what to do about Monsieur and Madame, however, or what not to do. They could see him nodding patiently at Monsieur's explanations. Finally Monsieur grasped his arm and literally sprang with him towards Blue and Geoff. Blue stepped out of the car and the introductions began. The girl, as they already suspected, was Thornleigh's daughter and her name they found, was Barbara. The Thornleighs had heard only that morning of the storm flow in Spinifex Creek and had grown anxious about the old Frenchman and Madame, so had decided to come on through Cantilla and find them.

"You seem to have a habit of getting Henri out of bits of bother, Geoff," Thornleigh laughed. Geoff might have replied that Monsieur seemed to have a habit of getting *into* bother and that he had paid for one rescue with a super-sports car. However he decided that that story could wait. But Thornleigh was speaking again.

"Well, now, I understand you chaps are going to Cantilla. That will be quite far enough for Madame, and Henri has had about enough for one day, too. It's a pity, rather, though, because I could get them a more comfortable sleep in Burramoola."

"Burramoola?" Geoff said quickly.

"That's right. That's our home town, so to speak. My place is about 200 miles west of there."

Geoff and Blue looked at each other. An animated conversation had been going on beyond them between Madame and Barbara Thornleigh, the joey sitting cheerfully erect and apparently enjoying every word. But, for some reason, both the excited voices fell silent together. Geoff spoke.

"Two hundred miles west of Burramoola, you say, Mr. Thornleigh? Well, in that case, I'm afraid you'll have to put up with us for neighbours for a little while. There's . . . it's rather a long story, as a matter of fact, but it must be out somewhere just beyond you that we're going. You'd be just east of that limestone country out there. It's the limestone ridges we've come to have a look at. As I say, it's a long story, but, for one thing, we think we might find gold there."

"Gold? Gold in the limestone country?" Dick Thornleigh shook his head. "Then I'm afraid, boys, you've come a long way for nothing. Those ridges are bad country whichever way you take them—waterless, bare, and, so far as minerals are concerned, utterly useless. As a matter of fact I've never heard of a gold find, big or small, within 500 miles." Then suddenly he laughed. "However, it's your business, boys, and it begins to look as though I'm trying to scare you away. On the contrary, I want you to come out to Matoorlie as my guests and, if I can help you, I'll be more than pleased."

The invitation was spoken with a quiet sincerity that his hearers were to learn was characteristic of big Dick Thornleigh. Again Geoff looked across at

Blue and his friend answered his look with his rare smile, obviously well content to let Geoff decide the matter. The latter turned back to the speaker.

"That's more than friendly, Mr. Thornleigh. But we might be out there six months. We've got a pretty complete outfit and we're used to the back country. We reckoned to buy a few horses and, if you'll let us camp on your property near water that will make all the difference. It's getting water out there that'll be our biggest bother, I guess."

"It's very nearly all my bother," Thornleigh answered, a little bitterly, Geoff thought. Then the tall man was chuckling again. "Very well, that's settled, boys. You'll stay at the homestead till you make arrangements to suit you. Now I think we'd better get moving again. Barbara, I want Henri to come along with me. Suppose you travel with Marie and Geoff?"

"If that's all right with Mr. Mason and Madame," the girl laughed. Geoff glanced past her at Blue getting back into the Minton beside Dogfoot, then back at her laughing face.

"I think I could stand the strain for quite a while," he grinned, "provided you dispense with that Mr. Mason nonsense,"

"Very well, then, no more Miss Thornleigh nonsense, please. It's not the thing west of the 150th Meridian. May I come in with you, Madame?"

To her surprise, however, Madame did not reply at once. Geoff had turned to lift the bonnet of the Packard and check the radiator and oil. Madame looked first at Monsieur burrowing in the glove box in the instrument board for cigars to refill his case. She waited till he had found them and rolled away to Thornleigh's car. Then she laid a hand on Barbara's arm, waved the other with an inimitable curve of the wrist at the six inches of cushion showing on either side of her and lowered her voice.

"Look you, Barbara, *ma chère*. For eight days I am squeeze in front there beside Henri. I am so squeeze that three time, when he lose his cigar, I am alight before we find it. Yet I do not care to complain for Henri would grieve. But now, for three hour in the great heat I 'ave this seat all myself. I think I am expan'! There is still room for the wallabee *petit* of the good Dogfoot, yes; but for you, *ma chère*, do you sit with M'sieur Geoff!"

CHAPTER ELEVEN

MATOORLIE

"I CAN see you don't think much of my cattle, Geoff." Dick Thornleigh spoke with a quiet chuckle. Geoff lifted a sandalled foot from the rolled edge of a long, low, drinking trough, brimful of water from the Burramoola town bore. He looked at the speaker in some embarrassment.

"Why, Mr. Thornleigh. . ."

But the other continued to chuckle, leaning back to prop his elbows on the horizontal pole set over the long trough. Some thirty or forty two-year-old steers, all red and white, were drinking from the trough, their noses deep in the clear water. About 150 more had finished drinking and moved off through the dusty gateway at the far end of the trough yard. They moved away slowly, patient and voiceless, as is the way with cattle "settled down" by weeks of travel. Dogfoot and Blue stood beside Geoff and Thornleigh at the trough and Monsieur somehow balanced his spherical form on the edge of the trough and puffed at a cigar.

It was ten o'clock on the morning after the meeting on the plain and already the party in the three cars had driven the fifty-eight flat miles from Cantilla to Burramoola. Even so, their departure from Cantilla had been delayed a little, for Monsieur had risen early to wash his car and had casually backed the green Packard into the bar-room of the little wooden hotel. The bar-room had been occupied by one hard-drinking stockman in search of a cure for a hangover. The stockman had yelled and set off for the Gulf of Carpentaria 500 miles away and it had taken the entire hotel staff to convince him that a green elephant hadn't come for him at last. However, the damage to the flimsy bar had been paid for (the Packard seemed to have sustained none at all) and they got away. Now Madame was resting at a Burramoola hotel, Barbara with her, while the five men inspected this small mob of Thornleigh's bullocks on their long trek to the south-east.

Geoff had been looking over the cattle with keen interest and some surprise. Though used, as he had said, to the back country, he had not been so far out as this before. He had heard that these stations raised big herds but sold them always in store condition (that is in lean condition) to the eastern cattle owners. But these were the first "saltbush" stock he had seen. The drinking steers at the trough were something of a surprise to him. They were all young animals and big framed for their age, with flanks showing full feeding and a gloss to their skin that told they had never known starvation. Yet not one of them was fat, or even approaching prime condition and there was a lankiness about them that puzzled him. It was the puzzlement in his face that had amused Thornleigh.

"You can't account for their ranginess, can you?" he continued. "A lot of people can't, who see our stock for the first time. You see, except for about one season in seven, this country doesn't fatten. It builds well-boned stock, due to the calcium content of the soil but in most seasons the herbage, saltbush especially, lacks the sugar needed for fattening. So, as soon as they're well grown we sell them east as stores. But our store cattle are much sought after because when they're turned on to the rich, sugary pastures of the eastern runs they top up very fast. Two men on the Darling Downs buy every hoof I can send them and they'd buy three times the number, if I had them. I haven't, worse luck—not these days."

He broke off as a stockman came through the big gate before them leading what was obviously a half-broken bay colt. He included them all in a friendly nod but he spoke only to Thornleigh.

"Two hundred and thirty one, all safe this far, Boss."

Thornleigh smiled.

"Good, Jim. You're not giving them to the dingoes, I see. Well, the two Government bores past Michenelly have been fixed, Grant tells me, so you'll have a straight drive. The cattle look nicely settled down."

"Too right, Boss. We got 'em so tame they come an' yarn to us round the fire. In fac' Jake's teachin' a couple o' the smartest ones to read an' write. Well, they've swallered as much as they can o' this bore so I reckon we'll push on to the next." He turned carelessly to his restive colt.

"Watch that fellow, Jim," Thornleigh said quickly. "You're not as young as you used to be. You ought to leave him to Jake."

"Aw, there's no harm in him at all, Boss," the stockman laughed. Already he had slipped the bridle rein over the head of the sidling horse. He drew the left rein short, faced the colt's tail put his left foot in the stirrup and lifted his weight by it. It is a mount that, nine times out of ten, ensures that a horse will step across under his rider. If, on the other hand, he jumps away, the man has his right foot still close to the ground. But Jim Fawkner made a careless mistake. He let his boot slide right home in the stirrup. Had the horse come to him, all would have been well. The big colt didn't. What happened next happened in little more than a second. Geoff saw the big horse jump sideways. In the same instant Jim Fawkner was hanging head down from a foot on to which the near stirrup had locked hard. The man's head and shoulders actually pounded the ground as the horse gathered his powerful haunches and flung forward. But that was not all. The now maddened colt was lashing savagely at his helpless burden, his swishing hoofs missing the man's head by inches. Already he had plunged through the gateway.

But a lithe form had sprung through the gate with him. Dogfoot's long arm flashed out and he grasped the stirrup leather high up on the saddle. A lightning twist and jerk and the leather was wrenched from its hook in the saddle tree, the horse was clear of his burden and clear away, and the man he had tried to kill was rolling over and over in the deep dust. The stirrup iron swung from its long leather in Dogfoot's hand.

But, before the others reached him the stockman

was sitting up. He shook his head, then put up a hand to the plaster of velvety dust on his face. Willing hands helped him to his feet.

To be "dragged in the stirrup" is the one predicament the stockman dreads; the one from which there is almost no hope of escape. Jim Fawkner stood swaying a moment, then the dust on his face actually cracked as he frowned heavily round.

"I'm dead, ain't I?" he asked, querulously. Thornleigh nodded sideways at Dogfoot, who had tossed the stirrup and leather at the foot of the gatepost.

"This chap—jumped after the horse—got to him and freed the leather, Jim! Best imitation of lightning I ever saw!"

Jim Fawkner turned deliberately and looked at the big black. He knew blackfellows. To some, as to some white men, he would have offered money then and there; but he didn't offer it to the bearded giant before him. Instead he held out his hand.

"Might be one day me catchem bad-one horse blonga you," he said quietly. It seemed an inadequate speech with which to thank a man who'd saved your life. But Fawkner knew Dogfoot would understand he was offering friendship, as between man and man. Then they all turned as another stockman galloped up.

"Good lord, Jim, I just seen that bay devil runnin' loose! You should have let me. . . ."

"An' now y' seein' me 'avin' me mornin' dust bath." Jim Fawkner growled. "Y'd think eight 'undred mile from the flamin' coast a man could count on a bit o' privacy! Anyhow, tell Billy and Tailor to run that bay down before he rolls on me saddle an' then he better saddle me somethin' nice and kind. He'll find me at the trough doin' me face up."

He shook hands with the party and walked away somewhat shakily to the trough, pulling off his shirt, from which the dust fell away in handfuls. Thornleigh stood still awhile and looked after him, unsmiling.

"He's had a bad shake-up but he'll throw things at us if we tell him so. I think he'll be right though, and I'll tell Jake to watch him for signs of concussion." With Monsieur, he led the way across to the tree under which he had left his car. The trio followed.

"Now, look here," Blue grumbled. "This rescue business is getting monotonous! One of you keeps on rescuing people out of cars. Then Dogfoot starts pulling 'em through train windows and proceeds to detaching them from bolting horses. It's time it stopped!"

Half an hour later the three cars were once more on the road, for the party hoped to reach their journey's end well before nightfall. Monsieur had again looked reproachfully at the Packard on account of the incident of the bar-room. He was even more surprised at her, he said, for never before had she pushed in the side of a bar-room submerging herself in splintered planks and sending an inoffensive drinker at full gallop across a saltbush plain!

"'Owever, she will, perhaps, be'ave for you, M'sieur Geoff," he said sadly. "I go to talk with

Deeck." So once more Geoff found himself in the Packard with Madame and Barbara.

For the first ten miles Madame talked gay broken English to Geoff and Barbara and torrential French to the joey. The joey seemed intensely interested and listened with ears widespread. The fussing over he had received from Madame and Barbara had filled his cup of joy. Clearly he'd had no idea there were so many fine people about, people you could really admire. He braced himself in the corner Madame had given him and looked cheerfully out on the world.

But the long journey and the continued heat were at last proving too much for Madame. Geoff, his eyes on the dust-cloud of the Minton a quarter of a mile ahead, was suddenly conscious that something was different. Then it dawned on him that no more French poured from the back seat but only a sound that was certainly not French. He flung a quick glance over his shoulder and grinned broadly. Barbara looked at him inquiringly and he jerked his head backwards. She turned and then giggled; for Madame slept peacefully, her mouth open wide; and, apparently the joey liked her immensely in repose, for he was leaning towards her, tilting his head to admire her the better.

"The poor dear!" Barbara exclaimed softly. "They shouldn't have come out here at this time of the year for the heat really is dreadful; but Mother and Daddy were afraid to be too emphatic for fear of misunderstanding. And Daddy is delighted to have M'sieur. Aren't they perfect darlings, though? I went to stay with them often when I was at school in Brisbane and I know." Geoff looked at the girl's smiling face.

"Hmph! I think that just about describes them," he grinned. Then he was looking ahead again to where the saltbush seemed to be giving place to a dreary waste of sandy country sparsely covered with spinifex grass.

"Well, look at that! We seem to have been travelling over saltbush for ever. But we've come to the end of it."

"There *is* an awful lot, isn't there? Yes, we run out of it now for a long way. This spinifex belt ahead is nearly a hundred miles wide. But we come to the saltbush again. Our place, Matoorlie, is mostly saltbush which makes it practically a drought-proof property so far as herbage is concerned. There are five stations out on what is known as the 'inside strip' of saltbush country. That is to say, we have four other stations as neighbours, within fifty miles of us. But Matoorlie's the worst off of all, now, for stock water."

"Bore shafts choking up?"

"Oh, no. The trouble is that the four bores we have are right at the northern end. That means Daddy can't use more than a third of his grazing except for the few weeks in those years there's rain water in the clay-pans on the south side. And this year and last we've had no rain. Not a drop."

"Yet the saltbush carries on?"

"Oh yes, it does. That's why I say that run's drought-proof so far as fodder is concerned. And that's why it's such a blow to be short of stock water."

Geoff swung the wheel a little as the big car sloughed into a patch of pure sand.

"And how about boring on the south side in the centre of the station? No luck?"

"None at all. Two contract men tried and failed and though Daddy paid their expenses, no more would come so far out. So Daddy bought a boring plant of his own and he's sunk shaft after shaft but it's been no use at all. It just seems that, except for the bores we have on the northern boundary, there just isn't any sub-artesian water on the place."

She was suddenly silent, then turned to Geoff as though she had made a decision.

"There's a little more to the story. Up till three years ago Daddy had the lease of land extending to the northward and he was given to understand that he could renew the lease when it ran out. It was because of that promise that he settled out here at all. But when the northern lease expired three years ago, Daddy's application was refused and the lease was given to a Mr. Matthews. We've found out since that Mr. Matthews knew nothing of Daddy's application and in any case if he hadn't got the lease someone else would have, as the Land Board considered Daddy had enough. So he has, if it were well watered, as he pointed out, but two-thirds of it is little use because of that, and yet because of the expenses of sending cattle so far east, big herds are necessary for we can never get better than store prices."

The Packard eased down as they approached a pot-hole, then picked up speed again in response to Geoff's foot on the accelerator.

"In that case Mr. Thornleigh has put a lot of money into a property that can't be adequately watered . . . was more or less misled into doing so?"

"I'm afraid it's too true. If Daddy sank a dozen bores near the four we have we'd be no better off, because as you probably know, cattle can travel only about ten miles to feed and back again to water. In very bad summer weather, duststorm weather, they can't do that, and they hang around the bores where there's nothing left for them to eat and lose condition very quickly." She laughed. "You see I'm a cattle-man's daughter. But I'm terribly sorry for Daddy. He's so proud of Matoorlie and the homestead he's made there—so are Mother and I. Now he's badly worried for he's been forced to sell off over half of his stock. That herd you saw at Burramoola this morning is the last of our full-grown bullocks. And I know that Daddy can't see how what we have left can even pay the station's expenses."

Geoff nodded. "How about piping water south from the bores you have?"

"Daddy's gone into that too, but he's given up the idea. He's laid the water on to the homestead from what we call Number Two Bore, a quarter of a mile away, but piping it miles across the run is another matter."

"Hmph! You'd be 500 miles from the rail and a thousand miles from the coast. The cost of piping delivered out here would beat you, I can see that."

There was more than a little gratitude in the look Barbara gave him. He had certainly proved an intelligent listener. Next moment she was laughing.

"Well, that's enough of our hard luck story! Look, Daddy's stopping for lunch. Poor Madame, we'll have to wake her. Oh dear, it's dreadfully hot for her!"

But the sleep, then the explosion of Dogfoot's large red alarm clock and lunch in the shade of a mulga clump revived Madame vastly. So much so that when, two hours later, the three cars drew up at the Matoorlie homestead, she was ready to greet Mrs. Thornleigh in true French fashion and to exclaim her delight with the homestead itself.

Matoorlie homestead was by no means the small village that those on many big eastern stations are. That wasn't what surprised Geoff, however. It was simply that he had been expecting a collection of wooden structures roofed with galvanised iron, those terrible buildings so common in the west, that seem specially designed to bake their occupants alive throughout the long fierce summers, built, in short, of the very worst materials for such a climate. Instead, he found a big pisé bungalow and an orderly collection of adobe sheds. All were roofed with iron, certainly, but under the iron was a thick mass of some insulating material that Barbara told them later was fireproof. But there was a second surprise in the shape of carefully tended trees and native shrubs forming what was nothing less than a well-shaded park surrounding the buildings. They had evidently been chosen and planted with knowledge and imagination and, with the water piped to them from the bore, they had made a magical growth that had completely banished the pitiful bareness and harshness so often the dominant note in western homesteads.

When the cars drove up three blackfellows came hurrying from the big garden where they had been working and there seemed to be quite a staff of lubras in the kitchen of the house itself, or rather grouped excitedly round the side door of it. A tinkling of hammer on anvil came from a shed beyond which was evidently a smithy, but it stopped and a stalwart blackfellow came to the doorway. Two native stockmen stood near it, one of them holding a broken piece of a windmill strut as he stared across at the cars. Geoff noted his fine physique. No desert myall, that chap, but from one of the north-east tribes, he'd bet on that. Barbara had told him that Thornleigh had employed fourteen native stockmen, but three of them were away with Jim Fawkner, and Jake.

But now the boy was out of the car and he and Blue and Dogfoot were introduced to a small woman, grey-haired, but with the same laughing mouth as Barbara's. They were all taken at once into a big summer-house, a sort of additional room detached from the house proper and some twenty-five feet square. It was so cool after the outside heat that Geoff exclaimed about it and Madame reverted to French and a vast deal of hand-play. Ice-cold drinks from a kerosene refrigerator completed Madame's ecstasy.

It was only after considerable discussion that Blue and Geoff persuaded their hostess and host that they would be well cared for by Dogfoot in their tent which they proposed to pitch in the cool shade of a heavily leafed York gum some fifty yards beyond the smithy. One thing, however, they accepted gladly was the use of a shower and bathroom attached to the two rooms usually occupied by Jim Fawkner and Jake, the other white stockman.

They promised to spend the evening at the house. Geoff puzzled about the matter of taking Dogfoot with them but decided to leave it to Blue. He was glad he did.

"Dogfoot," Blue said as the three sat in the dark outside the tent, "we all go longa big house, makem talk."

The answer came so promptly Geoff could have sworn the big blackfellow had had it ready.

"Me no savvy white feller talk, Boss. More better me sleep."

CHAPTER TWELVE

LAND OF DEVILS

GEOFF MASON and Dick Thornleigh sat their horses and looked across an expanse of low, reddish ridges that flung up a fierce glare and stretched away to the western horizon. They were ridges impossible to count, strangely set in rings and half rings, one within another. It seemed to Geoff they might have been a sea-bed of ooze thrust writhing and boiling into the sunlight and suddenly turned to stone.

Thornleigh's black pacer moved restlessly as though the hot, bare rock troubled her feet. The cattle-man steadied her with his left hand on the bridle and his quiet voice broke the silence.

"You see what I mean, Geoff? How many ridges can you see from here? Fifty . . . a hundred; and there are hundreds more further west and north. Any one of them might be the one your uncle's half-finished sketch map referred to. Mind you, I think you're right in coming, my boy. If you can discover where your uncle made his find of gold or whatever it was he did get, you may come on evidence that will bring those scoundrels to justice. In addition, there is no doubt your uncle wanted you to have the gold he said is still there—gold or whatever it is. But now you know the job you're up against; and I wouldn't blame you if you gave up the idea here and now."

Geoff nodded, lifted his hat and settled it again on his perspiring forehead. Already he had learnt that the quiet man beside him talked sense. To search that wicked tangle of limestone ridges for a crevice used for a den by dingoes, might take him and Blue a year and they might be no nearer finding it at the end of that time, for looking down he saw that the hoofs of the horses he and Thornleigh rode hadn't even scored the marble-hard surfaces. . . . A dingo lair! . . . One thought had been in his mind since they had ridden into the ridges. This south end of Matoorlie was waterless. The ridges also were waterless and they stretched twenty to thirty miles west of here. Dogs would make no hideout on this side of the desolation.

"How about dingoes, Mr. Thornleigh?"

The cattle-man leaned and ran a hand along the arching neck of his pacer.

"Oh, none to speak of. A few come in over our eastern boundary but they find enough wallabies to keep them from getting too hungry and we've lost only an occasional calf. Jim Fawkner did say once last year he thought there must be a pack settled in near some bit of a soak over west of the limestone; which makes me think the ridges you're looking for might be on the western side for, if there's one thing I'm certain of, it's that there's no water in these ridges. We made very sure of that when we came out to Matoorlie eight years ago and we found them so hopelessly barren I doubt if one of us has bothered to ride this far in among them at

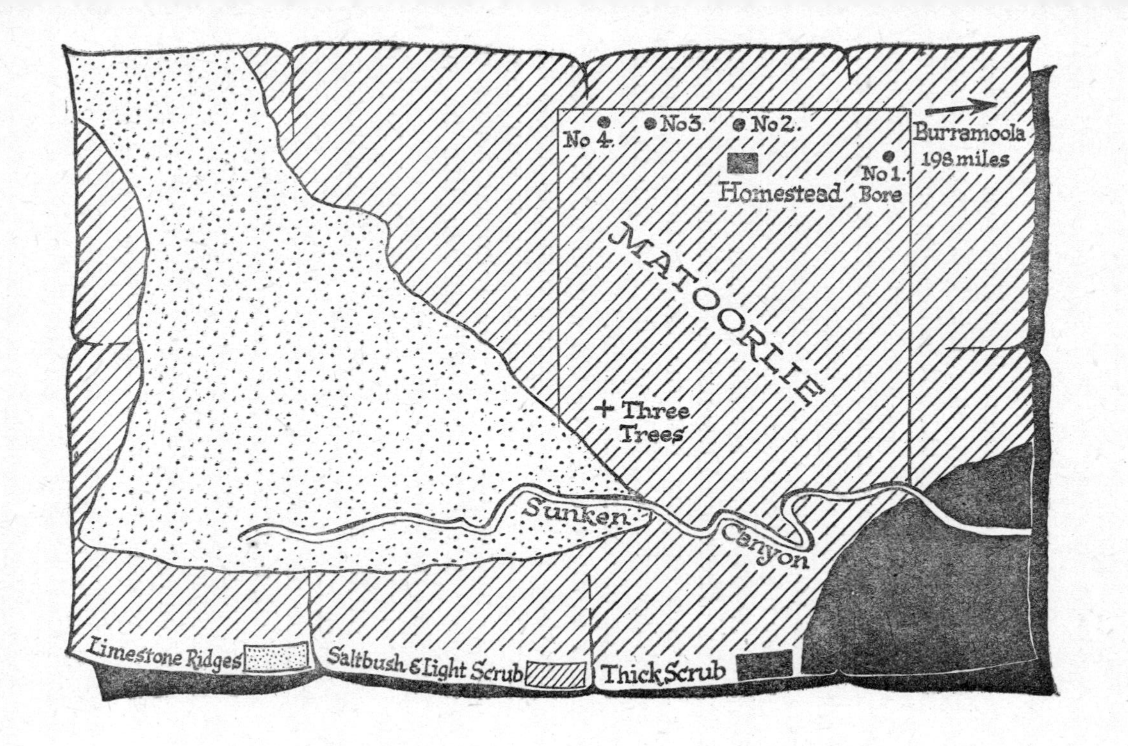
No 4.
No 3.
No 2.
Burramoola
198 miles
No 1.
Bore
Homestead
MATOORLIE
Three
Trees
Sunken
Canyon
Limestone Ridges
Saltbush & Light Scrub
Thick Scrub

any time during the last five years. What's more, even the myalls seem to find it a lot more interesting to stay on the western side."

Again the quiet lad nodded. Here was Thornleigh confirming his own surmise. Well, that narrowed the search a whole lot. But he had one more question.

"How about surface water Mr. Thornleigh? Does it lie on the rock or in any of the valleys after rain?"

Thornleigh shook his head.

"As you know limestone holds water very well—where it's not cracked. But it's the very devil to crack and consequently a sizeable sheet of water can't form. There are little inch-deep basins in the valley floors after rain but the evaporation in here is unbelievable. Within three days of rain there's not a drop of water left in sight."

"I thought that'd be the way of it. Now there's just this. If Uncle George had come out across here it's a wonder he didn't find his way to your homestead—follow that track we followed across the station. It's faint but a bushman like he was couldn't miss it."

"If he had malaria badly enough Geoff, he could ride within a hundred yards of the homestead and not see it."

Geoff nodded thoughtfully.

"Well, that's what I reckon, but I wanted to know what you thought, Mr. Thornleigh. And I reckon the one idea in Uncle George's mind would be to push on east, carry on due east. And the homesteads are few and far between, out here. . . . Well, perhaps we'll never know."

A girl's laugh came up to them and both men

glanced back to where Barbara and Blue and Monsieur rode towards them along the easy slope. Geoff and Thornleigh waited, saying nothing more, till the others ranged round them. Geoff's eyes twinkled at Monsieur's very uncertain seat on his staid mount. Indeed it was the old Frenchman's evident intention to fall off that had kept Blue and Barbara riding close on either side of him and had delayed them. But it was his remarks to his steed that had made Barbara laugh.

"'E is ze 'orse of unexpected undulation, Deeck," he said cheerfully. "Always one part of 'im rise up when I think it will descend!"

Thornleigh chuckled, then glanced at the sun.

"I don't trust you on a horse, Henri, and if you fall off on to this limestone it won't do you any good at all. Anyway, an hour in these ridges is quite enough for you and me. We'll leave the youngsters to it, and get back to the car." He turned to the others. "You're quite certain you don't want me to send the car back for you? It's thirty miles from here home, you know."

"Don't send it for us, Mr. Thornleigh," Geoff said. "But how about Barbara?"

"Tuppence will prefer to ride, I know, the tomboy!" Thornleigh laughed. "Well, it should be pleasant enough when the sun goes down, and your horses have been led out, so they're fresh. Micky the Tinker will bring ours on home. All right then. But I'd get out off the ridges before dark, if I were you. If a horse happens to slip and fall you might have trouble."

"*Mon Dieu!*" Monsieur gasped. "It is ze land of

ze devil, surely! I am so 'ot, soon will I be ze dried meat and *mon cheval* also! *Mon Dieu*, 'e turn 'imself about! 'E is ze 'orse of great sense!"

Amid the general laughter, Thornleigh and the old Frenchman started back. For a minute Barbara and her escort looked after them through the red glare flung up by the fire-hot ridges. Blue slipped from his saddle and tightened the girth a hole, then unscrewed the top of a small canvas waterbag strapped to a set of saddlebag dees. He unstrapped a tin mug, rinsed and filled it.

"Anybody like a drink?"

The others were glad to accept but Geoff handed back the empty pannikin rather absently for again he was looking out across the ridges. The limestone ridge land sliced across the south-west corner of Matoorlie. Geoff was looking due south and he was frowning now. Twisted and tumbled though they were, the ridges were low, with easy slopes. Only here and there did a slope sweep up steeply, like the side of a swirl in a boiling cauldron. But, half a mile to the southward, he could see what certainly looked like a cliff. He turned to Barbara.

"What's that bit up there, Barbara?"

The girl peered from under her hat brim.

"Oh that's a bit of Sunken Canyon you can see. We call it a canyon for want of a better name, though it's.... But why not ride up and see it properly?"

"If it suits you chaps," Geoff said.

Ten minutes later the two boys were gazing in wonder from a cliff some sixty feet high at a similar cliff opposite them, the opposite wall of the canyon. The parallel cliffs seemed to run east and west without a break, forming a great trench cutting across the tumble of ridges and valleys. Blue was the first to speak.

"Well I'll go hopping! We've got all we want now to play injuns with!" He pulled off his hat, dragged down his mouth corners and scowled at Barbara, then tapped his red hair; "Big Chief Fire-on-Top," he grated. Then he raised his arm slowly and pointed scornfully at Geoff, "Little Chief No-Good-Cuss!"

Barbara spluttered, but Geoff had urged his pony closer to the cliff edge.

"Caesar, it's Navajo country, sure enough! Can you get across this thing, Barbara?"

"No, not anywhere. It's about seventy miles long, the men say. Its western end is about twenty-five miles from here but it winds eastward for roughly fifty miles. You can't cross it and you can't ride along it for it's blocked every few hundred yards by pieces of the cliffs that have fallen. But just over that ridge on the right you can get down to the floor from this side. Would you like to see it?"

"Sure," Geoff said again. "But hang it, this heat's the deuce. How much more of it can you stand?"

"Don't worry, I'm a Queenslander, you know. Come on then." She bent in the saddle and her pony moved off, stepping a little short as all the horses seemed to do on this smooth rock surface. Almost as good a surface for a car as for horses was Geoff's thought as they rode, even though that loose conglomerate would keep a car bumping like the deuce. He and Blue rode up on either side of Barbara and presently they crossed a ridge and turned along the floor of a little valley that swept down and down right to the bottom of the canyon. Right ahead now, Geoff could see the opposite wall of the canyon rising above their line of vision. And it would seem that the giant hand that had torn this gap in the nearer wall had clutched once at the opposite cliff. It was sixty feet high, but a breakaway had made a wide ledge sloping at thirty degrees, from half-way up the cliff to the top of it; and the ledge seemed, somehow, to turn into the cliff as though it would enter a tunnel in the sheer rock. But that was not all. Immediately to the right of where the ledge ended the cliff, for its full height, formed a great concavity, like part of the wall of a circular tower sixty feet high. It was into this concavity that the sloping ledge seemed to turn, rolling on its side like a banked road. Geoff reined in and stared.

"If you could reach that ledge . . . but not even a mountain goat could get up to it! What do you reckon, Blue?"

He turned to look over Barbara's head at his friend. But Blue was not there. He had reined in twenty yards back and was staring at the concave cliff. Geoff watched him a moment, then grinned.

"The feller seems interested," he chuckled. But now Blue was riding down to them. He was frowning.

"Nice piece of scenery," he commented. "Nice and hard!"

"Pity that ledge didn't come right down, instead of only half-way," Geoff said. "But it'd take a darned sure-footed lizard all his time to get up to where it starts."

Blue glanced at him, then back over his shoulder up the steep slope of the valley floor down which they had ridden, then once more across at the cliff.

"Ha!" he said absently. "Lizard, eh? Hmph!"

"Hmph! Lizard eh? Ha!" Geoff mocked. "Well, what do you think, feller?"

But his red-haired friend seemed to have lost interest in the subject. He took his right foot from the stirrup and swung his trousered leg over the saddle pommel.

"Better take a look at that sun, you chaps. If we're going anywhere else we'd better keep moving."

"That's so, the sun'll be down in half an hour," Geoff answered. "How about if we ride north-west from here, Barbara? That won't take us any farther from the edge of the plain and then we can sheer off to the right and start for home."

Half an hour later the trio dismounted and stood, bridle reins in hand, looking towards the setting sun. All about them were a hundred ridges that shone like burnished bronze, some almost straight, many twisted into grotesque, zigzag formation, others forming concentric circles. For a moment it seemed to Geoff that they writhed all together, like the surface of a giant cauldron of boiling mud. Then the sun's edge dipped and the shining bronze of the ridge crests was suddenly gone.

"Caesar," he said. "I reckon M'sieur isn't far wrong! This place is made specially for devils!"

As if to answer him, a terrible sound flung across the desolation—a devilish laugh that came louder and louder in peal after devilish peal!

CHAPTER THIRTEEN

THE CAPTURE

"BUT, DADDY, we all heard it! It was just awful!"

"All right, Barbara, I'm not saying you didn't hear what you thought was a laugh. But there could be an explanation. For instance, the wind plays tricks in rocky places. Do you remember Tom Cordy who worked here awhile when you were a nipper?" Thornleigh turned in his deck-chair to include the other listeners sitting in the dim lamp-light in the summer-house. "Well, Tom and I were camped with cattle on our way south through Birdsville and we had a bit of a stampede in the small hours that was caused by a blood-curdling howling that started suddenly way out to one side of the mob. The herd was pretty travel-wise and we didn't have much bother to get them milling but by the time we did it was daylight. We couldn't find anything to account for the unholy racket. But three weeks later, when we'd delivered the bullocks, we camped there again and hanged if we didn't hear the very same noise. We sneaked towards it in the moonlight. But we needn't have gone to so much trouble. It was a chunk of rock fallen across a gap between two boulders and the night wind whistling through the gap set up a long, sustained note like the pipe of a pipe organ, except that it rose and fell with the little gusts. Now. . . ."

"*Non! Non*, Deeck, *non!*"

Monsieur seemed to have sprung from his chair and his glowing cigar described a fiery circle as he pointed south-west, "It is the 'ome of the devil, I believe you. If you say you see 'im, also I believe you!"

"Well," Blue said quietly, "we certainly didn't *see* anything, M'sieur. We had a look round but there wasn't much time. It took us till dark to get out of the ridges as it was. That was how Geoff's horse came to fall. But Geoff and I are going out there to-morrow."

He stood up. "Thanks awfully for that supper, Mrs. Thornleigh. I'll push over to the tent now, and wait for Geoff and Dogfoot. Er . . . there's your cigar on the rail, M'sieur."

"Ah, *merci*" Monsieur answered, straightening from a search he was making under the table. He picked up the glowing cigar and looked at it reproachfully. "I cannot understan'. More and more when I set down ze cigar 'e disappear!"

"Very well then Blue," Mrs. Thornleigh said. "But I'll leave some supper for Geoff and Dogfoot in the kitchen. They shouldn't be long now, at any rate. It was near the Three Trees you left him, wasn't it?"

"Yes, Mother," Barbara answered. "Dogfoot should have got back to him nearly two hours ago. When Snip went lame we turned him loose and Geoff started walking home along the truck track. If Dogfoot follows the track he can't miss him."

"He won't. And thanks again, Mrs. Thornleigh,"

Blue said. "I'll tell Geoff about the supper. We're giving plenty of bother to-day. Good night everybody."

It was after midnight. In the dark as they left the ridges Geoff's horse had stepped on a loose rock that had thrown him heavily. Fortunately Geoff had sprung clear and when the horse had regained its feet it had seemed none the worse. It must have twisted its near hock, however, for within five miles it had begun to limp. Geoff and Blue examined its hock by the light of a match, and saw that the joint was already badly swollen. That meant, simply, that Geoff was afoot, for the Matoorlie horses were not trained to such indignities as carrying two riders and almost any horse can throw a rider mounted behind the saddle. There was nothing for it but for Blue and Barbara to go on and send back a horse for Geoff. The latter stripped his saddle and bridle from the lame horse and turned it loose and the others had left Geoff tramping along the track that led across the big run. They had pushed their horses and reached the homestead in a little over two hours; and within twenty minutes Dogfoot was on his way back along the track riding a fresh horse and leading another for Geoff.

When Blue walked the two hundred yards from the house to the tent the moon was well up. He could see through the homestead trees and across the dusty plain to where the huts of Dick Thornleigh's native stockmen stood in a clump nearly a mile away. They were a cheery lot, not myalls, but Wakelburra blacks.

"They're more contented, living well away,"

Thornleigh had said, chuckling a little. "For instance, Jimmy the Tinker likes to crack his Nellie on the head now and then with the heavy end of his stockwhip handle and he can do it over there without worrying about what Mrs. Thornleigh will think of him. Nellie makes a bit of fuss at the time but she wouldn't dream of bringing tales to the house about him."

The stockmen had lost no time in making Dogfoot's acquaintance. They had begun by inviting him to help them with a day's work. Dogfoot had come to Blue the night before.

"That one Micky the Tinker catchem horse longa me longa sun up, Boss."

"Okay, Dogfoot, you go longa Micky," Blue had said. He suspected the big fellow had been hankering for sight and sound of his own people. So Dogfoot, mounted on a Matoorlie stockhorse, had ridden off with the others at daybreak to the eastern end of the run. Blue and Geoff gathered that the stockmen had to go out daily now and force the cattle south as far as practicable, for the saltbush on the northern side near the bores was nearly all eaten out and the stock, mostly cows and calves and yearlings, were losing condition fast. If it didn't rain soon, Thornleigh would certainly be up against it. It hadn't rained for two years but a two year drought was no novelty out here. Blue had heard of aborigine children five years old who had never seen rain. No wonder Thornleigh was worried. Well, as for Dogfoot, he must have had a chummy day for he and his pals had already been exchanging gifts. Apparently the stockmen did a little wallaby spearing to get a change from beef, and they'd given Dogfoot about a dozen spears. Dogfoot, for his part had given Micky the Tinker his umbrella. But he had gone farther than that, much farther. He had bestowed upon the camp his middle-sized alarm clock to be used, it seemed, on a community basis, each hut to have the pleasure of the clock's ticking and the delight of its alarm on consecutive days. The big black had brought the spears home, tied in a bundle.

Just as Blue sat down on his bunk in the tent he heard hoof beats. He frowned. The sound was of galloping hoofs! Good heavens! Geoff would never be so discourteous as to force his host's horses at full gallop on a hot night!

Then he knew it was one horse only he heard, and presently he could see it, and its rider, too. The rider was Dogfoot standing in the stirrups and riding hard!

Blue heard voices behind him, then the sound of the side garden gate opening. Then Dogfoot was reining his horse back on its haunches and had jumped to the ground. But the big black spoke coolly.

"Me no findem Mister Geoff. Findem track boot blongs white feller. Findem car track. White feller bin carry Mister Geoff longa car."

CHAPTER FOURTEEN

"WHERE ARE THOSE OPALS, MASON?"

When Geoff recovered his senses he was lying on the floor of a utility truck, his ankles tied and his hands tied behind his back. In time with his pulse beat, sharp pain stabbed at his temples. Through half-open eyes he could see the low sides of the truck in the light of the moon just rising, and he could feel the roughness of a tarpaulin against his cheek. Then he snapped his eyes shut as a man walked round the tail of the truck.

"Heck, he's still out to it!" a voice exclaimed. "You muster 'it 'im pretty 'ard, Don!"

"He'll come round."

The new voice had a bitter edge to it that Geoff remembered easily. It was Graster's. "It saved no end of trouble and here he is."

"Yes." Geoff could tell that the third speaker was angry. "I notice you haven't got the map, though. You were mighty sure he carried it around with him and he'd have it on him."

The first speaker laughed uneasily and Geoff decided that he was Redshirt, upon whom he had opened hostilities at the gorge.

"You was lucky you didn't find 'im with a gun ready, Don. I still wake up surprised to find I ain't a bloomin' sieve! An' Dirk didn't swap shots with 'im either, that day at the gorge. 'E muster forgot he had his automatic with 'im!"

"You talk too much Lakker," the other growled. "You know well enough he was right out of range and——"

"You both talk too much!" Graster snapped. "Get up in the back with Mason, Ben. You'd better put something under his head, I suppose. Now, start up, Dirk. That Redhead and the girl are out of hearing by now."

Geoff felt a hand grasp his hair and a folded blanket was pushed under his head. Then, as Lakker climbed in and sat beside him on the floor, the two cab doors snapped shut together, the engine started and the little truck lurched away. The running was easy enough at first, but not for long. The truck slowed a little presently, swung right, heeled over and almost at once a bumping began. Geoff knew then that they had turned in among the ridges. The bumping and lurching were the wheels striking and skidding over the loose conglomerate. Without the makeshift pillow, he would have lost consciousness again in the first mile. He knew why Graster was crossing the limestone. They would work along west for the twenty-five miles necessary to get round the end of Sunken Canyon, then once out of the ridges to the south of it, turn west, perhaps. But, after half an hour the truck stopped and Graster got out. He stood a moment, looking in at Geoff.

"Well, young Mason, how do you like it?"

"So it's you Graster, come to see if I'm dead. Do you think you can get away with this, you fool?

Anyway, to begin with, I'm darned thirsty. Give me a drink."

The other laughed, then thrust a hand in his shirt pocket and drew out a box of matches.

"Yes, I thought that crack on the head would make you thirsty. And you're going to stay thirsty till you talk. Being thirsty is nothing at all to what's coming to you. Think it over!"

He struck a match and held it close to Geoff's face but said nothing more. He blew it out and turned back to the cab and Geoff heard his trouser legs swish together as he climbed in. The truck lurched on once more.

Geoff's thirst was real enough, brought on, as Graster had said, by the savage blow that had knocked him out. That would be the way Graster had hit Uncle George. The pain in his head had actually eased a little, however but the lurching and bumping made it impossible for him to think clearly. Then, when he thought he could endure the nightmare no longer, it ceased quite suddenly and the truck was running on soft, level ground. Having rounded the canyon and travelled south they had left the ridges at last, and turned west again.

He glanced at Lakker, now curled, like himself, on the floor of the utility; then up at the moon, well up in the north-eastern sky. He raised himself a little and peered over the side of the truck just in time to see a mob of scrub wallabies thumping away in the moonlight. Then he lay down again and forced his dazed mind to grapple with events.

. . . Apparently Graster had been scouting the south-west boundary of Matoorlie, his truck hidden in the ridges. Even so the riding party must have almost surprised the scoundrels. But, when Graster saw Thornleigh and Monsieur ride away he had seen his opportunity to get Geoff and, as he hoped, the map. It was risky, for he must have known the Matoorlie people could phone the police at Burramoola; still, it was no easy matter for the police to corner a man in this country and Graster would work fast once he learnt what he wanted. Graster and Dirk must have gone ahead to the Three Trees while Barbara and Blue and Geoff were still out among the ridges—a tramp of probably ten miles but the last part of it in the dark, most likely. They must have intended a hold-up. The horse going lame had saved them the need for that but at least it had saved Barbara a bad fright, too. As for tying up Blue and Barbara, Graster would know Thornleigh would come looking for the party if it was late returning. Letting them go would give Graster actually more time and it was much safer.

Geoff looked out again at the moon and saw they were travelling west still. It would be slow work for Dogfoot and Blue, tracking the truck through the ridges. It might take them a day, unless Blue and Thornleigh guessed the direction Graster would come. More probably Blue would decide to drive or ride through, then search the southern edge of the ridge country for tracks. That would be the best plan, but it would still give Graster a good many hours' start.

The boy cursed his own carelessness for not being ready for a move like this. After all, it was about the only one Graster could make. And now the thing had happened that he'd wanted all along to avoid—Blue and Dogfoot would be running into serious danger. Blue, as he himself admitted, was a poor hand with a gun. He and Dogfoot were no match for these swine, yet they wouldn't wait for help from the police, he knew well. He cursed again. Graster would never believe he and Blue had come right out here on the strength of information so meagre. He had found no map on Geoff but he would feel certain the boy would have learnt many details from his uncle, and he intended to have them. There was a chance to set him on a false trail, but not much of a chance. Graster was no fool.

His brain refused to think any longer and he dozed. When he wöke, daylight was in the sky. He looked at Ben Lakker, still curled asleep beside him. The truck was still running on saltbush but, by the feel of the wheel drive, the country was more sandy; and they had made one more change of direction, turned south once more, confound it!

Just then Lakker woke too and sat up sleepily and Geoff felt the truck slow down and vibrate to a gear change. After that, for perhaps ten minutes, branches of scrub swished over them and shut out the light. Then they were out in the bright light of a clearing. The truck stopped.

"So far, so good," he heard Graster mutter as he and Dirk got out of the cab. Ben Lakker was already climbing over the tailboard.

"Get a fire fixed, Ben, and see it doesn't make much smoke. The redhead and the blackfellow will be a day's travel behind us but that black can see a long way, like all the rest of them, curse him.

Untie Mason's legs, Dirk, and prop him against the desert gum facing the sun."

Dirk grunted something and obeyed. The untying of his ankles brought vast relief to Geoff, though he had already thanked his stars that, instead of shorts he had been wearing trousers and socks for the ride the previous afternoon. As for his wrists, he had managed to strain the lashings a little, enough to permit circulation; but his arms ached cruelly from being kept so long in the one unaccustomed position. With Dirk's aid, he walked to the tree and sat down with his back to it, his still bound hands twisted a little to one side. Without a hat to protect him, the early sun flashed hurtfully in his eyes but he was able to twist his head sufficiently to get relief from it most of the time.

He had already seen that he was in the middle of a clearing some two hundred yards wide, the little desert gum behind him being one of two very stunted trees in it. The second tree grew some ten yards from a tent on the other side of the fire Lakker had started. Apparently Graster was using this clearing as a hide-out, for there were signs that the party had camped here for some days. Geoff could see across the clearing and a little way into a tangle of wilga trees and "desert oak," a kind of whip-stick shrub with green needles for leaves. He twisted to watch his three captors getting breakfast. Ben was managing the fire skilfully for, a few feet above it, what little smoke it had made thinned and disappeared. For some minutes Dirk moved about stiffly, obviously still in a very bad humour. Presently he poured water in a dish and sluiced noisily, though without even removing the shoulder holster of his automatic. Graster had gone straight into the tent. The smell of frying bacon stabbed through the warm sweet air of the clearing.

At last, at a call from Ben, Graster came out of the tent, a rifle in one hand. He leant the rifle against the truck, then took the plate Lakker offered him. He took no notice whatever of Geoff till he had finished his breakfast. Then he strolled across, and faced Geoff, thumbs hooked in his belt.

Geoff looked him full in the face and it seemed to him that the tigerish cruelty that leered out of this man's eyes was something he had never seen before. He wondered how his uncle had come to have dealings with such a man. But men who knew the Inside and were prepared to take on a tough prospecting trip were hard to find, he supposed, and his uncle had taken a risk with him. Graster was a killer; but one who killed only if he thought it safe and who, as often as possible, got his killing done for him. But Geoff knew now he was worse than that. He was a devil; a devil who would shrink from no sort of cruelty; on the contrary, he would enjoy inflicting it. Geoff jerked his body up a little. He did not wait for Graster to speak.

"Come to start the Third Degree session, Graster? All set to enjoy yourself, you hound! Like you enjoyed leaving Uncle George to die of thirst and malaria—or thought you did."

It was guesswork, the result of his suspicions, but he saw at once from Graster's face, that he had guessed aright. He saw Ben Lakker look up sharply, set down the dish he had filled and walk across. Dirk had come to the left of Geoff and was rolling a cigarette. He paused in the act of licking the gummed edge and looked hard at Graster as Geoff continued.

"But you missed out didn't you. The man you deserted came out with a big haul. When you found that out and caught up with him you robbed him, or thought you did, but you were wrong again. You took the wrong box. And then you killed him. But now you still want a map, don't you? When you saw me take a paper out of that box you were sure that was it. And that time you were right. But you'll never see that map Graster. I burnt it!"

"What!"

While Geoff had been speaking, Graster's thin lips had drawn back like a snarling dog's. He took a step forward.

"That's right. Burnt it, Graster. So what, you hound?"

Clearly, neither Dirk nor Lakker had expected this defiance. Geoff, his senses keyed for the battle of wits he knew was before him, felt certain he saw a queer satisfaction in the eyes of both. His enemy saw it too. He stepped close to Geoff and smashed his fist into his face deliberately. The blood from his split lips tasted salty on Geoff's tongue tip. Blood coursed down his right cheek from a deep cut under one eye.

"That's just to go on with, Mason," Graster said thickly. "So you know about the opals. Of course you do. That was why I brought you here. You say you've burnt the map. You're lying. But you'll know what's in it by this time and you're going to tell me—and a lot besides!"

Opals! Geoff kept his eyes on Graster while blood dripped slowly from his chin. So it was opals Uncle George had brought out! That made it easier to understand why Graster had finally got news of his find. A man with gold to sell could have sold it to a bank and no information would have been given to outsiders. But opals would be different. They were tricky to value in the rough. But Uncle George was a sick man when he got out and he would have to have money. Yet he hadn't sold his horse. Old Toby was back there on the farm now. That meant that almost certainly Uncle George had persuaded some storekeeper or publican to risk an advance on some uncut opals. But Graster was speaking again.

"Tie his ankles, Dirk!"

Dirk stepped back slowly to the truck table where he'd left the rope.

"You're not moving fast enough, Maddon!" Graster's voice was low and hard-edged. It seemed to do something to Dirk Maddon for the man's lethargy left him and he was back in a moment, jerked Geoff's feet together and whipped the double cord twice round his ankles.

"Now, Mason, here's where we start. Where are those opals?"

His lips were set in a thin line as his left hand grasped Geoff's hair and jerked back his head. At the same moment he crouched and punched with his right. It was a terrible blow. Geoff, already fighting thirst, the gruelling of the journey and the pain of his split lips, felt his senses reeling. He clenched his teeth and, as through a fog, he heard Graster's voice again.

"Where are the opals, Mason?"

He ran his tongue over his bleeding lips and forced himself to speak, though his voice was hoarse.

"You can't get away with this, Graster. You——"

A fist crashed into his mouth again. "Take that Mason. And you wait—I'll find a way to *make* you talk." Graster walked the half dozen paces to the fire, took up an iron rod, and dropping on his haunches beside the fire he thrust it into the coals. . . . There was a sudden, high-pitched, swishing scream, a clink as of hard wood striking metal, and a queer, crunching thud. The iron rod flew from Graster's hand ten feet in the air; and a long-shafted spear was quivering in the centre of the banked fire!

CHAPTER FIFTEEN

THE PURSUIT

BLUE CAMPBELL looked at the big blackfellow standing still in the moonlight beside his panting horse. The message was clear enough. Some white men had carried Geoff to a car.

"How many white feller?"

Dogfoot held up three fingers.

"Me bin follow 'im track blonga car. Car, 'im go longa rock ridge." He pointed south-west. Blue heard quick strides behind him and Thornleigh was at his shoulder.

"What's the trouble, Blue?"

"Dogfoot says he can't find Geoff. He came on the tracks of three white men and a car. They drove into the ridges."

Thornleigh wasted no time on exclamations.

"It'll be that Graster scoundrel. Well, if they've struck into the ridges they'll take the shortest cut through them, I'd say. That's round the western end of Sunken Canyon and then south a little into the saltbush again and light scrub country. But that'll keep them in the limestone for twenty-five miles and it will take them over three hours. Still, I'd say they're through it by this time."

Blue nodded.

"It's a good five hours since we left Geoff, and I

can't travel any faster through those ridges than they can. Allowing for stops to pick up their tracks that gives them six hours start." His face was serious as he spoke. "I don't like it much, Mr. Thornleigh. That Graster hound has already set his gunman on to do Geoff in, and he won't hesitate to use any sort of Third Degree methods to get what he wants out of him when he finds he still hasn't collected that map; and kill him when he's made him talk, if he thinks it's safe. . . ." He broke off as Barbara came running across the garden.

"What is it, Daddy?"

Thornleigh told her briefly but Blue already turned to Dogfoot.

"We go longa car blonga Mister Geoff."

The black nodded quickly, then wheeled and moved off with long strides, leading his blown horse. Blue turned back to Thornleigh and Barbara.

"I can save time by going east, round the eastern end of the canyon, if the country's fairly clear of scrub." But Thornleigh shook his head.

"It's not clear of scrub, Blue. South-east of my place you run into scrub that'll keep you down to a walking pace for thirty miles and the same returning on the other side of the canyon. No, the only way is through the ridges, the way the scoundrels have gone. We'll ring Burramoola police but it'll take Grant and Wallace a good six hours to get here. We'd better get away now and try and locate Graster and his crowd, anyway."

Blue looked at him unsmiling.

"I'm not pulling you into this bother any farther than I can help, Mr. Thornleigh. We're giving you enough trouble as it is. Geoff would be darned sore with me if I let you in for any more."

"But, good heavens, my boy. . . ."

"You won't change my mind about it, Mr. Thornleigh," Blue said quietly. "Now, I'd better get going."

By this time Monsieur had joined them and Blue found Dogfoot topping up the radiator of the Minton. Willing hands filled the petrol tank from the big drum mounted on its stand and wheeled the car from the shed. Thornleigh carefully stowed two small drums of petrol in the boot, though the car's tank held enough for nearly three hundred miles. Blue sent Dogfoot to the tent for Geoff's rifle, the shot gun and the automatic. Barbara looked at him, tight-lipped, as he gave the black his instructions, then ran back to the house. Blue and Dogfoot had the same habit of moving unhurriedly, but with amazing swiftness. He surprised Thornleigh now by jacking up the car's rear wheels. The Minton carried two spare wheels as yet unused. Almost before the petrol tank was filled they were on in place of the two slightly worn ones and the latter were on the big rack behind. Then Blue was going round all the tyres, pressure gauge in hand.

"Would you mind letting the hood down?" he asked Thornleigh. The cattle-man and Monsieur complied.

"You've got my idea of it, I think," Thornleigh said as he bent over the hood. "They've gone round the western end of the canyon, then south a bit to get off the limestone. After which they could go south or swing west, but I don't think they'll go east. They wouldn't get far enough into those scrub belts. I'll be surprised if they don't turn west, once they leave the ridges. There's very little timber along the south-western corner of the limestone country."

"Anybody living out there?"

"Not a soul. There was a station away to the west but the soaks weren't enough and only one of the bores they sank was any good. Between water shortage and a good deal of cattle spearing by myalls, they pulled out about eight years ago."

When Blue stood up at last, Dogfoot had come back and Barbara and her mother had come from the house with two big boxes of provisions. Madame came behind them. In addition to the guns and ammunition Dogfoot carried seven spears, apparently selected from the bundle given him by the stockmen. He put them in the car, their butts to the floor under the panel, and leant them back over the seat. Blue looked at them once only, but it seemed to Barbara that the quick look softened, for a second, the hard-set lines of his poker face. But next moment he was getting into the car, motioning the black in beside him.

"Ah, M'sieur Blue, we will pray for your safe return," Madame said. But Monsieur appeared to have another thought in mind, just then.

"Shoot ze leg, M'sieur Blue! I 'ave experiment on ze Boche. Ze leg, 'e is 'ard to miss, an' your man 'e cannot stand without 'im!"

Blue's smile flickered as he replied.

"Thanks, M'sieur. Well, so long, everybody."

The big engine sprang to life and he answered

the chorus of good-byes with a wave of the hand. Then the Minton's headlamps blazed out and she was swinging away through the homestead trees and on to the track that led south-west across the station.

The speedo needle moved up and up but Blue didn't seem even to notice it. Graster probably wouldn't start his devil's work till he had got right back to his hide-out. But his six hours' start would be all he'd need. Yet, there was no chance, even with this car, of reducing it by more than an hour. To drive fast through the ridges would simply mean a wrecked car. The saltbush plain whipped away under flying wheels while her slight-built driver kept steady eyes on the white light, flung far ahead. And his mouth was a hard line. Yes, there was *one* chance to use the Minton's power! To cut Graster's lead by more than half!

Nearing Sunken Canyon, Dogfoot touched Blue's arm. Blue slowed at once, peered and saw where car tracks swung to the right from the plain. He swung right too and nosed the long-bodied sports into the first of the shallow valleys between two ridges. They traversed the valley, then Blue swung the car left, along the slope of a ridge. Again Dogfoot touched his arm and pointed right. Blue shook his head. The Minton topped the low ridge and her headlamps slashed across the little valley that Barbara had shown Blue and Geoff before sunset and, in two hundred yards, the car had reached the last steep slope before the valley swept down to the floor of the canyon. In the blaze of white light from the lamps, the lower half of the sixty foot cliff showed glistening red. The upper half and the sloping ledge to the left of it were lit only by the moon till Blue pressed the dispersal switch. Then the whole of the wall, concave cliff, ledge and all showed clear. He cut the engine and at once the silence of the desolate land closed round them.

But Dogfoot looked quickly at the boy by his side. Suddenly he straightened, strong fingers of his right hand tight-gripped on his bundle of spears. Many times he had looked down, one of an awed crowd, and watched this lad send a powerful motor bicycle roaring round and round the vertical walls of a cylindrical tower. Ten, twenty, thirty feet up, wheels and the boy's body at right angles to the sheer walls. The centrifugal force that held them there was an unfathomable mystery to Dogfoot. He grew to hate that great wooden cylinder and the ear-splitting roar of the big machine. To him, every ride was a baiting of the Evil Spirit, bringing beads of sweat to his forehead as he watched. Yet he had seen Blue make that ride many times in a day, and day after day. But in the end he had seen the Evil Spirit strike; had seen the heavy machine flash up and over, hang sickeningly in the air, then, still roaring, crash down on the helpless rider. He had sprung through the door into the fume-packed arena and lifted it from his friend's twisted body. Now, before him, red in the blaze of the headlamps, was this concave cliff, like half of that great cylinder he had hated! He knew now what Blue intended! His voice, deep like the bass note of an organ, was breathless and hoarse as he bent towards his friend.

"No! . . . No Boss! . . . You no do!"

Blue turned at the urgent words and looked into the bearded face; into the deep-set eyes filled with entreaty. Then suddenly his rare smile softened the hard lines of his face.

"You good boy, Dogfoot!" he said softly. He hesitated, as though searching for more words that would be understood by this simple giant who loved him above all else. He looked again at the earnest face. Then he was speaking curtly again, pointing down the slope. "You help me pickem up stone. Quickfellow!"

He stepped out briskly, moved to the rear of the car and unscrewed and lifted off the two spare wheels. Each one rang musically as he bounced it gently on the limestone. Dogfoot turned his head to watch then, lifting his bundle of spears, he too was out of the car. He laid down the spears, strode forward, stooped and commenced throwing aside the few loose stones between the car and the floor of the canyon. Blue came forward and joined him and together they worked down to the canyon bottom. Blue tested the sprinkling of grit on the rock floor with his foot, then crossed it and laid a hand to the slope of the cliff where it sloped up ten feet before the fifty feet of sheer wall began. He felt the surface with his finger tips. Then he looked at Dogfoot and jerked his head.

"Leavem big rope in car—takem out gun, water-bag, tucker box, petrol drum."

He followed the black up the slope but walking slowly now as though to save his breathing from quickening. When he reached the Minton Dogfoot had the guns on the ground with his spears and the other things close by.

Blue opened the door, got in and started the engine. He leant out sideways and seemed to sight along the long, tapering bonnet that housed the twelve murmuring cylinders. For a full minute he stayed, leaning out. Twice his head tilted as his eyes travelled slowly up the concave cliff and down. Then suddenly he straightened and turned to Dogfoot a yard away on his right. Once more his rare smile made his teeth flash in the moonlight.

Next instant his feet and hands moved, quick, sure movements that almost seemed one motion only, and the big engine's murmur was suddenly a roar that shattered the limitless silence. Hands and feet moved again and, as though awaiting their touch, the great car shot forward. In yards, on that steep slope, she gathered headlong speed and flung herself down it. The air screamed past her wind glass. The cliff ahead towered up as though to spring upon her.

To Dogfoot the next seconds were hours. He saw the long, sleek bonnet fling upwards as the front wheels took the out-thrust of the cliff's foot; saw the car tilt perilously sideways, twenty feet up, yet her wheels seemed glued to that curved wall, her roaring engine filling the canyon with thunder. Already she was half-way across the curve on the concave wall. She swept up higher, higher still, as high as the ledge; she had crossed the curve of the cliff; her front wheels had reached the wide twist of the ledge, spot-lighted by the lamps. . . . But there she seemed to hang, her wheels slowed till he could see their turning, her engine's roar gone, replaced by a laboured growling. The momentum that had flung her up the cliff face was all but spent; the force that pressed her to the wall would hold her there but an instant more!

But for that perilous instant Blue's hands had been waiting. He changed gear in a flash—right down to low. The engine roared again, the rear wheels took the twist of the rock face from cliff to ledge; they were on the ledge itself, their new tyres biting the sloping rock of it, the twelve pounding cylinders, flinging their thunder once more up and down the canyon, were fighting the terrible drag of the void, fighting it and out-matching it. Slow-turning wheels kept turning, ten feet, twenty; ten feet more.

Then the front tyres were over the canyon rim, over and beyond it, the long car level and rolling to a stop, the engine roar gone, sunk suddenly to a murmur that was swallowed with the echoes in the silence.

CHAPTER SIXTEEN

BATTLE TACTICS

BLUE GOT out and stood beside the car's fenders. Then he leaned in again and switched off the headlights. He saw his hand was trembling now and smiled grimly. This was how he'd been after his first wall ride, he remembered; and, after the last one, he had thought never to make another! But what a car she was! It was that gear change that had worried him, the change right back to low; and she'd taken it and fought out under full throttle! What a thoroughbred she was!

A deep-throated shout came from down in the canyon and Blue strode the few yards to the brink and waved to Dogfoot. The big black was looking up and laughing, his teeth showing white.

"Me sendem down rope, Dogfoot. You tie 'im longa that one wheel, longa 'im tucker box."

Blue returned quickly to the car, opened the boot and dragged out the heavy tow rope he had brought. He braked the car hard, chocked the rear wheels and then tied the rope to the off-side one. That done, he picked up the coil, carried it down the ledge, paying out carefully as he went, and ran the slack over and down the remaining thirty feet of cliff to Dogfoot. The black lashed one article after another for Blue to pull up and finally climbed the rope himself.

In less than five minutes the gear was stowed and

they were in the car seat. Blue had donned a coat and Dogfoot also, for the night was cool at last. As the Minton moved off Blue glanced at his watch. Five to two. They had reached the canyon at twenty to two. Now they were across it and the crossing had saved them at least three hours slow travel in the ridges. The job now was to make the most of that and, if possible, to catch up another hour.

For a quarter of an hour he listened for any engine or transmission noise that would suggest that the Minton had suffered damage. There was none. They were still in the ridges, identical with those across Sunken Canyon but, within two miles, the white shaft of the headlamps stabbed down from a ridge top on a level stretch of saltbush. They ran down on to it and felt the big car riding smoothly once more. Blue swung her away to the right, heading west.

His plan was simple. He would drive west along the southern edge of the limestone. It would be daylight by four o'clock. By now Graster might be a hundred to a hundred and fifty miles to the westward. They couldn't overtake him by dawn but they must get as far as they could. As the Minton gathered speed a little mob of wallabies leapt, one after the other, through the light beam and thudded away to the left.

Twenty minutes later both men jerked upright, together, then Blue slowed the car and stopped it. There, clear in the white beam of the powerful lights, were tyre tracks!

Blue's heart lifted. He flicked open the car door and stepped out quickly, Dogfoot with him. Tyre tracks, sure enough, and ones that could have been made by the utility they had seen lurching away from the gorge four days ago. But Dogfoot was already striding to the right. Thirty yards away he turned and beckoned to Blue. When the latter reached him, he saw what he had found—a second set of tracks.

"That one car come longa this way. 'Im go back this way longa moon 'im come up."

Blue looked hard at the black. Dogfoot was telling him that that car had gone back over its own tracks at moonrise. He had long ago discovered that the black could tell with amazing accuracy how old a track was. But Dogfoot had stepped back into the white light of the headlamps. He waited for Blue, then pointed almost carelessly at a long scratch that crossed a tyre track. The mark of the tread was not broken by the scratch. It showed clear upon it, which meant, of course, that the car had driven over the scratch.

"Wallaby 'im bin scratchem all about longa moon 'im come up. Car 'im chasem wallaby."

Again Blue looked at him. A car had scared away a mob of wallabies at moonrise. But he still didn't know how on earth Dogfoot was so sure of the time. Well, it was no use trying to find *that* out. The moon had risen just about midnight. Now it was nearly half past two. Then, if Dogfoot was right, Graster had no more than two and a half hours' start! He must have made slow work of the ridges or else he felt pretty safe and wasn't hurrying! He wheeled and stepped briskly to the driver's door of the Minton and the black strode to the other door.

"Good," Blue said. "Now might be we catchem. We go quickfellow. You watchem track."

He started the engine, let in the clutch and, with a quick twist of his lithe body he settled to drive.

Many times in after years Dogfoot was to live over again the next ninety minutes when he sat with the English boy he had seen dice with death once more and win. The tracks ahead showed clear in the headlights. He saw the speedometer needle swing up and up till it quivered between a seven and a nought and the miles and minutes flung away together; the night air screamed over the windshield and the great engine sang its song of speed. It seemed to him at last that the song had gone on for ever, yet still the flying wheels skimmed the moonlit plain!

But at long last Blue eased the throttle. When he did the engine note changed to a sound that was somehow strange and hushed. The big car drew slowly to a stop and the plain that had been flashing beneath them seemed to have come to rest, silent and wide.

He switched off the headlights, then pointed away to the left, at a bluish smudge of scrub that reached away southward. It was no island of trees such as they had passed again and again, but a wide belt that seemed to stretch west and south. To the north was no longer the tumbled skyline of the ridges but now a continuation of the plain they were on. The tracks still led away ahead, almost due west. But to follow them farther would be merely to warn armed men of their coming or to drive into an ambush.

He looked at his watch. A quarter to four. It would be daylight in less than half an hour. Graster might not be more than twenty miles ahead. He might even be holed up in that big scrub belt away on the left there. It would be better to swing south, now, follow the scrub. At least that would screen them once daylight came and if they found nothing they could come back here. He let in the clutch again.

But he drove now at easy speed for, as well as having the lights off, they had reached a definite change in the surface of the plain. Every now and then he felt the rear wheels slip in sand patches and the saltbush was giving way to patches of spinifex. The scrub stretched away south for nearly five miles, then they swung west once more.

It was plain day, with the east turning fiery, when Blue stopped the car beside a woolly-butt that thrust above the desert oak and wilga of which the rest of the scrub consisted.

"You climb that one tree, Dogfoot."

The hunter got out, strode across to the tree and climbed quickly into the upper branches. One foot in a swaying fork, a hand on a slender limb, he twisted to look east, north and west. It was only after several minutes scrutiny that he looked down and shook his head.

"Big mob wallaby that way—long way. Him all feed." He pointed north-west with a free hand. "No can see car."

Blue was frowning as he drove on once more. Graster's car or truck would very probably have set a big mob of wallabies on the move. Then either he hadn't got as far as that mob out on the plain or he had a longer start than they thought and the wallabies had settled down behind his truck to feed again.

When they had driven another mile the scrub edge swung again to the southward; but, instead of turning to follow it, Blue drove the big car slowly into the scrub ahead, its twelve cylinders ticking over almost noiselessly to the easy, level-ground load. He swung the wheel this way and that, ever watchful for the thinnest growth. Even so, now and then a supple branch would swish over the wind screen and drag at Dogfoot's spears. There were no trees now, but only the scrub. For half an hour they snaked their way through it, then they saw the wilga tops turn to red gold. The sun was rising.

Again Blue stopped the car. He had to decide now whether to push on slowly like this or go back and follow up the truck tracks. The latter course would lose him much time and probably warn his enemies. But Graster might be fifty miles ahead and they were here wasting time after all—time he had taken a fearful risk to save. He glanced across at Dogfoot and his frown deepened, but with astonishment. The big hunter was no longer beside him. He had slipped from the car and dropped on all fours. In that position he was poised, tense, his head thrown up a little and his wide nostrils dilating and contracting! Then he bounded to his feet.

"Bacon, Boss! Him fryem!"

Long ago, pidgin English had ceased to be comic for Blue. He had heard more than one grim story told in its seemingly foolish phrases. But here was Dogfoot crawling about on hands and knees and then talking about frying bacon!

Now, however, the black was pointing north-east through the scrub and again he spoke eagerly.

"White man 'im cookem kaikai breakfus'. Him fryem bacon, Boss!"

Then Blue understood and was out of the car. The smell of frying bacon would carry much farther through timber than the smell of smoke.

"That way," Dogfoot said, a long arm pointing north-east again, and there was the light of battle in his eyes.

It did not occur to Blue to doubt him. He leant swiftly into the car and cut the engine. He hesitated as he looked at the guns. The rifle would be of little use to him for he was a poor shot. It would have to be the shot gun. But he would take Geoff's automatic.

With its holster strap slipped over his head, he buckled on the belt of the shot-gun cartridges. Dogfoot was waiting, his spears loose in his hands, the long wommera grasped with three shafts in his right hand. Blue nodded and the hunter led the way.

The scrub grew thicker as they strode forward but Dogfoot, stooping and twisting, seemed to find a way with ease. They travelled perhaps a quarter of a mile. By then Blue could smell frying plainly, and then smoke, the faintly aromatic smoke of burning wilga. When he looked up it seemed to him there was more light off to the right—a clearing! He was about to speak when the black halted, crouched and laid his spears on the sandy ground by his knee. He looked up over his shoulder and beckoned to Blue. The latter crouched beside him and peered under a thick-leafed gidya shrub, peered eastward into a sunlit clearing, a tent showing white in the centre, a utility truck drawn up beyond and facing towards them. There was a fire to the right of it and two stunted trees. Three men stood looking down at the butt of the farther tree. One, a thickset man, wore an automatic in a shoulder holster. And then Blue saw what it was they were looking at; saw Geoff's right shoulder and his bound hands clenched and half-buried in the sand beside the tree butt. Suddenly the tallest of the three watchers crouched and swung his clenched fist. Then he had stepped astride of Geoff's legs and was slapping his face with fierce blows that had the weight of his body in them and Blue could see Geoff's head flung cruelly from shoulder to shoulder.

He threw the shot gun forward, then realised he was yet out of range. At the same moment Graster straightened, strode to the fire and picked up an iron rod. Blue started to scramble to his feet but Dogfoot's long arm pulled him down, then pointed across at the eastern side of the clearing.

"Boss, me sendem spear now. White man watch this way. You go that way."

Blue thought quickly. Graster was twirling the iron and speaking, Blue could hear his voice faintly but not his words. He flicked a glance at the hunter at his side. He had once seen Dogfoot transfix a kangaroo with a spear at nearly two hundred yards. The black could draw the fire of their enemies yet keep well in cover. He was proposing to do that while Blue worked round the clearing.

Without a word the lad got to his feet and moved swiftly away. He made good speed till he was half-way round, then he peered out again, and, for the first time he saw Geoff's face. He gritted his teeth and crouched, ready to spring into the clearing.

But in that moment he saw the spear flash out from the scrub on the west side. He could hear the whistle of it as it arched over, then, descending, it swept the rod from Graster's hand and drove deep into the heaped coals of the fire. The long shaft quivered, sloping a little from the vertical. As Graster's body jerked erect the iron rod fell to the sand, its heated end across a fragment of bark that sent up a little spiral of white smoke into the hot sunlight.

A shout burst from the other two men as Blue backed away and began the rest of his crouching journey round the clearing. They sprang forward beside Graster facing the west side, Maddon's gun already in his hand. Blue heard the automatic bark three times, then a rifle shot, then a whistling sound and a scream. He flung himself to the ground in time to see the small man dragging at a spear that pinned his left leg to the tree near the tent.

"Darned myalls! Get under the truck!"

The shout came from Graster above Lakker's screaming. As Blue scrambled on shot after shot rang out, cutting through the hoarse screams. He had seen two spears arch down and drive into the sand close on either side of the truck. He reached the clearing's edge in time to see one more flash in the sun. It glanced off the bonnet of the truck, struck the sand, then toppled forward, its shaft clattering down on a half empty drum beside the truck. Maddon, prone beneath the truck beside Graster, fired past a front wheel and to the right of the tent. In the same instant Lakker's screaming stopped and the man sagged sideways. His fall must have jerked the spear blade from the flesh of his leg but one trouser leg was still pinned to the tree.

But now Blue had broken into the clearing and was running straight for Geoff. He had no need to muffle his footfalls for, half-way across, there came a storm of abuse and more shots as two spears in the air together, crumped, quivering, into the ground each within inches of one of the truck's rear wheels. Before the fusillade of shots ceased he was beside his friend and Geoff, his face thick-coated with sand grains from his squirming on the sand, was staring up at him. Blue dropped the shot gun, whipped out his knife and, with an upward slash, severed the ropes on Geoff's wrist just as Maddon fired again from beneath the truck. Blue jerked the automatic from its holster and thrust it into Geoff's hand, then cut the ropes on his ankles. As Geoff came to his feet Blue reached and picked up the shot gun. Then they both moved swiftly but silently across to the truck

Graster and Maddon were still peering forward but no more spears whistled from the clearing's edge. The whole, wide clearing was suddenly silent. Geoff crouched quickly and his voice came like a whip crack.

"Drop your guns and back out!" But with the last word he fired three times, the automatic bullets whipping up a shower of sand between the two prostrate men. "If you turn I'll shoot you to pieces! And I'm not waiting!"

He saw the two go rigid. There was no mistake about the shots behind them, nor those bullets that had stung their faces with upflung sand. "He's as fast as they come!" they heard Maddon mutter. Then Geoff saw both men move together, squirming back empty-handed under the high-set back axle of the truck. He watched their every movement. As they came out he stood up and moved aside.

"Now, lie down! Face down!"

As they obeyed him, both twisted their heads to look at him. It was then that Blue spoke.

"Now take a look at my nice shot gun. I'll blow you in half and won't charge you!"

With his friend's angry words Geoff saw all hope die out of Graster's eyes.

"Okay, tie them up Blue," he said. As he spoke, a giant form came striding across the clearing, a single spear in his right hand. As he passed the fire he jerked the now blazing spear out of the coals and threw it on the sand where it lay smouldering. Geoff glanced at him once, then back at the men on the ground and stood without moving a muscle while Blue tied the hands of both and then their ankles. He had had to act too fast to voice his amazement at his friends' arrival—at their coming at sunrise instead of sunset! The question was uppermost in his mind now, but he thrust it away.

Graster and Maddon secured, he grinned at Blue and Dogfoot. It was a grin distorted by swollen lips but his handshake was firm. Then he turned quickly and stepped to the other tree where Lakker lay, still unconscious. The little man, in falling, had dragged the haft-end of the spear to the ground but the flint point was still wedged in the soft sapwood. Dogfoot freed it with a quick jerk. Blue slashed away the blood-soaked trouser leg and they inspected the wound. It was fortunate the spear had happened to strike the tree. That had prevented the tapering blade from severing the artery.

"That feller no stay longa one place!" Dogfoot said gravely, his frown and tone seemed to ask what one is to do with a person who gets fidgety with spears whistling round.

His answer was a shout of laughter. In fact it was a full minute before Geoff could speak at all. Then, still laughing, he looked at the big hunter. "So you pegged him to a tree till you could get round to him, feller!"

CHAPTER SEVENTEEN

THE RETURN

GEOFF LOUNGED on a tarpaulin in the shade, a mug of cooled tea in one hand. Graster and Maddon lay on the floor of the truck which, however, Blue had backed into the shade of the scrub. Lakker conscious now and with his leg tightly bandaged, they had put on the lighter tarpaulin, spread in the shade of the other tree. The Minton, her hood raised, stood in the shade of another tree behind Geoff.

Lakker's wound had called for proper attention. Fortunately a complete first aid kit had been packed for Blue with the food, and, while Lakker was still unconscious, Blue and Geoff had closed the gash and inserted five stitches. Now, having drunk a mug of tea, the little man was lying back, his eyes closed. Only his wrists were tied.

"Now, let me see if I've got it straight," Geoff was saying. "You crossed the Canyon! How you did that no one but yourself will ever know, son. Well, then you picked up the truck tracks and finally located us in this darned scrub thanks largely to Dogfoot. After which the old gazooker drew their fire while you came in behind 'em." He grinned at Blue. "That was a real idea, feller. Your Army training did you some good after all."

"Army training, nothing! Dogfoot had that one

worked out before we set things popping. He just seemed to take it for granted that was the thing to do. Must be one of the jokes his forefathers played on other jokers ten thousand years ago. Anyhow, you'd better stop jawing, son, and get some sleep."

"Sleep!" Geoff sat up with an indignant jerk of the head. "You'd think I was all set for an old ladies' home! Think my head can't take a bit of a crack? It's good quality bone, let me tell you and pretty near solid. In other words I'm ready to travel when you are, and the sooner the better because they'll be worried stiff at the homestead. Thank heaven these birds had this extra drum of petrol."

That point settled they discussed how they would take the prisoners. Lakker's deep spear wound would demand some care and they decided that the bumping in the tray of the truck would quite probably start it bleeding again and that the little man would have to be taken in the cab or in the car. Blue suggested that Geoff take him in the car but Geoff refused.

"The way you look at that car makes me nervous," he grinned. "You can pelt her up a thirty foot wall without even scratching her duco but I'm as likely as not to grate her gears or something any time, in which case you'd probably fall down in a swoon. But the sooner one of us gets back to Matoorlie the more trouble everybody will be saved, I reckon. You can make better time with the Minton on those ridges than I could. So you lend me Dogfoot and take Lakker and push ahead."

To that Blue finally agreed. They transferred Lakker to the big sports. The little man had no fight left in him. Indeed he looked very sick. Blue eased the rope and tied his hands in front of him. He sat in the car saying nothing and looking straight before him, his hurt leg propped on his bag of clothes.

Neither did Graster and Maddon say anything when Geoff and Blue lifted them out of the truck to spread the folded tent on the floor of it, then lifted them back. With Dogfoot's help, Geoff doubled the small tarpaulin and stretched it over the front part of the truck tray from the top edge of each side so as to make a shade for the men's heads. Tied up and without such protection, the sun would, he knew, send them mad. To make sure they could not undo each others hands and feet, each man's wrists were secured loosely to opposite sides of the truck tray. Their guns Dogfoot put in the boot of the Minton, then tied his retrieved spears along the side of the truck tray. The trio made a careful search of the camp but no papers of any kind were found among the gear and clothing of their prisoners.

"Okay, feller," Geoff grinned at last, when he and Blue had taken a last look round. "You'll cut into the ridges where the truck tracks lead in and get round the west end of Sunken Canyon." He glanced at his wrist watch as he climbed into the truck beside Dogfoot. "A quarter past eight. If not eaten by wallabies, you should make the homestead before four o'clock. But this truck's no flier. It'll take us an extra three hours."

"Right," Blue answered, but he scowled at the two prisoners in the back of the truck. "These useless swine should have been in Brisbane gaol these twenty years!"

He walked on and slipped in behind the driving wheel of the Minton, started her up and led the way through the scrub, the way the truck had driven in, and the utility lurched along behind. When both car and truck were presently in the open again Blue waved a hand and drove away. Geoff, too, increased speed, and soon both car and truck were far across the plain. But the Minton continued to draw away and within an hour she was out of sight.

And scarcely had Geoff and Dogfoot lost sight of her than the offside front tyre of the truck began to drag the steering. Geoff stopped. There was a spare tyre but when he examined it he didn't like the look of it and he decided to mend the puncture. It proved a long job for the wheel was out of true and jammed the tyre bead. Consequently before they came to where the tracks swung into the ridges it was after one o'clock.

The sun was savagely hot now and a fiery west wind was rising. The four hours crossing the red ridges would be fierce enough. So Geoff decided on a quick meal, Dogfoot freeing the hands of one prisoner at a time so that he could eat. Then once more they got going.

The hot wind increased in strength, the fierce red glare of the ridges seemed to increase with it. Twice the engine boiled as the tilted truck toiled up a ridge side. Geoff kept going, however, and, at last, with vast relief, he saw from a ridge top the grey-green of the saltbush plain on the eastern horizon —the south-west corner of Matoorlie. As the truck churned along in second gear he glanced away northward. Lord, what a wicked tangle these ridges were!

A queer set-up! Nothing could possibly live there—nothing! That laugh they'd heard. . . . Funny none of the Matoorlie people had ever heard it. But Thornleigh had said none of the Matoorlie stockmen ever rode into the ridges. There just wasn't anything to go there for, and probably the myalls stayed out for the same reason. Blue said Thornleigh thought there must be some simple explanation of the mad laughter. Probably there was; but not wind! Hang it, that ghastly sound could never be made by wind whistling among rocks! The fact was he'd . . . he'd heard that laugh before. But heavens, no! That would be impossible!

Well, to-morrow or next day they'd cut in and ride across westward. And they'd take Dogfoot.

An hour later, the saltbush was in plain sight; but as the truck lurched up and on to a ridge top, Geoff felt the black's hand on his elbow and turned to find him pointing across to the left. Apparently Dogfoot wanted him to stop. He drew the truck to a standstill and at once the black stepped from the cab and ran down the shallow valley on their left. His eyes puckered to the glare, Geoff stared, astonished that he had not seen it before—a dingo with two strong-legged cubs at her heels was two hundred yards along the little valley and springing away up the opposite ridge side. As Dogfoot approached, she galloped ahead, then halted and wheeled. One of the cubs followed her easily up the slope and Geoff marvelled that its feet were so soon hardened to the hot rock surface. The other cub, however, was lame, very lame. He struggled gamely but the two were on top of the ridge before he was half-way up. For a moment, as the black ran towards him, the mother dog watched his battling, obviously torn between his need and the danger to the other cub. Then in a flash, she wheeled, the cub with her, and vanished over the ridge.

The lame cub seemed to know he had been forsaken, for he set up a piteous crying that came downwind to Geoff, then redoubled his efforts. But, yards from the ridge crest, he fell over and rolled down. He sprang up and battled on again and this time he was almost over when a second time he lost balance and rolled back down the slope, right into the stooping giant's hand.

Geoff grinned as his friend straightened. Trust Dogfoot to spot that cub in trouble! But how the deuce could he walk barefoot on that sun-heated rock surface? But now the black was staring downwards, not at the cub but, apparently at the rock. For a full minute, holding the cub in one hand, the big black stood silhouetted against the hot sky, the searing wind rippling his khaki shirt. What was he waiting for? Then he was striding back down the ridge, across the little valley and up to the truck. He came round to Geoff's side and with a flick of the wrist he tossed the little dingo cub over and caught it again, feet up, then grasped its right foreleg in his right hand. Geoff got out and looked at it. He saw the cause of the cub's lameness, and, while the black held the paw he took out his knife and, between thumb and knife blade, drew out an inch-long needle of limestone driven deep between the toes. Apparently the splinter had driven in only a short time before, because the paw was smeared with blood. The cub's only protest was a soft whining as though he were grumbling to himself, but the operation must have relieved him of much pain for at once he lay still in Dogfoot's hand. But he arched his neck and his small forehead puckered in a frown of bright-eyed puzzlement. Dogfoot looked up at Geoff, his eyes holding the eager look Geoff had learnt to know. He seemed to take a breath.

"Mudder blong 'im. . . ."

"Now look here, feller," Geoff laughed, and then remembered to talk pidgin. "Okay, you fetchem that one cub longa truck. You leavem here, might be him killem dead." (To a blackfellow, if someone is merely "killem" he is merely injured or sick. If he dies he is "killem dead.")

It was possible the dingo would return and find the cub but, with the other to get to safety, there was no knowing, and the cub could never find his way out of here by himself. That dingo had known where she was going. He looked at his watch—just past five. She might be on her way through the ridges to a soak she knew beyond them. Her cubs were old enough to travel twenty or thirty miles in a night. She might have come last night from the station bores in the north, lain up all day in the light timber belt across there in the saltbush and was on her way again now. She certainly couldn't have a lair near here for there was no water.

He looked again at the cub. The little fellow was

thirsty but he wasn't in a bad way. Still his mother would have suckled him before she left cover. Yes, that would be it, no doubt, and she was out to cross the ridges to the west. That confirmed his idea that it would be on the west side of the limestone they'd find the ridge of Uncle George's. Then another thought struck him. This cub. They might be able to use him for a decoy when they reached what they thought was a likely location. It was worth keeping in mind!

But already Dogfoot had set the cub on the cushion of the cab. And just then Graster's voice came from the truck tray.

"Lord, Mason, give us a drink for God's sake!"

Geoff glanced over the truck side at the prisoners. A different Graster this to the swine who'd had him in his power less than twelve hours ago. He turned and looked east to the saltbush plain a mile away.

"We'll be out of the ridges in a mile," he said. "I'll give you a drink then."

Ten minutes more of twisting and bumping and with a sigh of relief Geoff drove out on to the saltbush. His watch showed a quarter past five. He stopped the truck and stood by, gun in hand, while Dogfoot untied Maddon and handed him a water-bag, then secured him and untied Graster. Both prisoners were bound again and Geoff was pouring water from one bag into the truck radiator when a grunt from Dogfoot made him look round. A small dust-cloud to the north-east whipped away low by the wind, told him a car was coming up the track that crossed the big station.

"Boss," was Dogfoot's laconic contribution, and

sure enough, it was the Minton. But, instead of a trooper, as Geoff expected, Blue had Barbara with him. He drove up alongside the truck.

"Mr. Mason, I presume," he said and held out his hand gloomily. But Barbara was looking at Geoff's swollen lips and cut face and she seemed to have forgotten to speak at all. Geoff grinned what he imagined was a cheerful grin but it didn't seem to cheer Barbara.

"Oh, *Geoff*!" she said.

Then Blue cut in. "Why was he born so beautiful? Why was he born at all?" he asked plaintively. Then: "Oh, my gosh!"

For, at that point, the dingo cub, apparently tired of being alone, suddenly somersaulted out of the door of the cab and picked himself off the saltbush plain with the glad surprise of one who has done something a lot more complicated than he thought he could. This time Geoff laughed heartily and the sound seemed to reassure Barbara. She laughed too, jumped out and picked up the woolly cub.

"Oh, isn't he a *darling*! Oh, and look at his poor foot! Where did you get him, Geoff?"

"I didn't," Geoff laughed. "Dogfoot found him."

"No!" Blue whispered hoarsely, but he looked hard at the cub's paw, the pad of which was swollen. "Get the thorn out?" he asked gloomily. Geoff laughed again.

"You old fraud!" he said. "You know darned well you'd have brought him home yourself. Well, how's everybody? Sorry I've been the cause of such a darned lot of bother, Barbara. And, by jove, it's jolly decent of you two to come out to meet us."

"Mr. Thornleigh would have come but he's had to ride out and make some arrangements about the stock on account of this hot wind," Blue said. "But that reminds me. Barbara's got to be back in an hour from now, or else! So get going, feller—get home and disguise yourself in a clean shirt. I'm ashamed of you!"

Geoff had noticed him glance at the rear of the truck when he had first driven up, and he had stopped the car where Barbara could not see the prisoners. Since then both boys had been careful not to mention them. Now Blue was out of the car and was climbing into the cab of the truck. Geoff's protest was drowned in the roar of the revved-up engine and the slam of the door as Dogfoot, dingo cub and all, slipped in on the other side beside Blue. The latter kept the engine roaring till Geoff, laughing, had swung the Minton and driven away.

CHAPTER EIGHTEEN

GRASTER'S NERVE FAILS

"IT IS ze fast work!" Monsieur said. "In eighteen hour to, what you say, bring 'ome ze bacon, tied up tight, *mon Dieu*! And ze good Dogfoot, 'e remember to shoot for ze leg, Deeck! With ze Boche it never fail. Every time, *je vous assure*, 'e bite ze mud! Yet, for ze so small Lakker I am grieve a little. 'E is not young man and 'e 'ave much pain. Ah, *merci*, *ma chère* Barbara!"

Monsieur took a tumbler from the tray Barbara held, a tumbler that glistened, ice-cold, in the lamplight. Having drained it, Monsieur peered cautiously round the summer-house. Barbara laughed as she relinquished her tray to Geoff.

"You must have finished it in the study when you went for your paper, M'sieur."

"Ah, that will be it, surely," Monsieur said. The others laughed too as he reached happily for his cigar case. He drew out a fresh cigar, cut it and lit it carefully. He held it between thumb and finger, then drew a sheet of paper towards him, a little white powder upon it.

"I 'ave examine this limestone as you ask me, M'sieur Geoff. 'E is different, this one. 'E is like marble yet 'e is 'arder than marble! That is strange, *mon ami*." Geoff sat forward, his face full of interest.

"I understand limestone is nearly always a sea-bed, M'sieur; and I've got a theory that those ridges are a sea-bed made terrifically hot by some convulsion and suddenly hoisted up while it was, well, sort of boiling. But how could heat like that affect, say, the sandstone underlying the limestone?"

Monsieur laughed so heartily that he dropped his cigar and Blue had to retrieve it from under Thornleigh's chair.

"But, M'sieur Geoff, if we could say that, we could find ze gem by thousan'! But no man can say. Ze silica in ze sand, 'e might become isolate as chalcedony, agate, opal, jasper, bloodstone. . . . 'E might. But no man can tell if 'e will do a 'undred things!"

"By jove, M'sieur!"

Geoff would have liked to continue the discussion but he glanced at Thornleigh and paused uneasily. His host, he knew, was worried and had had a hard day and the anxiety about Blue and himself hadn't helped. The hot westerly to-day was bad for the stock, for they needed more water under such conditions. The wind had gone down with the sun but the night was stiflingly hot and the westerly would certainly get up again to-morrow.

The police, they had discovered, would not be out till next day, for Grant, the Sergeant, had just been transferred and his relief, a man named Calwell, had not arrived. The other trooper, Doug Wallace, could not leave Burramoola till Calwell came. So Graster and Maddon, when they had been fed, had been tied up again for the night and shut in the saddle shed that stood by itself on the side of the homestead towards the horse yards. Lakker had been put to bed in a little skillion room that adjoined a machinery shed, and, except for the smithy, the building nearest the tent. Lakker's leg had grown very painful and the little man could not attempt to walk. Madame and Monsieur had promptly taken over the care of him. He sank back on the pillow of the bed Madame made up for him as if a bed, just then, was about all he was interested in. Geoff, Blue, Thornleigh and Monsieur had had a last look at Graster and Maddon and then returned to the summer-house.

Geoff, leant back, drained the rest of his drink and then stood up. Blue stood up with him and slid his glass on the tray.

"We're Public Nuisance Number One round here," Geoff laughed. "It's time we let you people get some sleep." The two said good night and walked across to their tent. In ten minutes they were in bed and asleep.

In the saddle room three hundred yards away Graster sat erect, peering through a small window. The dark shed was heavy with the fragrance of a cigar and Graster held the gleaming stump of the cigar in his right hand. But, with his left, he bound his right wrist loosely with rope, then stubbed the cigar and thrust his left hand through the loose rope loops so that his wrists seemed tied together. Then he lay down again.

"They're putting the lights out in the house," he whispered to Maddon. "Half an hour will do. And Mason and that redhead will sleep like logs."

His guess was correct. But, if Blue and Geoff were all in, the Thornleighs and Madame and Monsieur had had little enough sleep either, since Geoff's capture. In less than half an hour the house was quiet. Graster listened a little longer for steps that would warn him of a last inspection by any of the menfolk. Then he sat up once more and whispered to Maddon. Beginning with the burnt ends, both men unwound the ropes from wrists and ankles and stood up in the darkness.

"They didn't bother to lock the door," Graster said. "Yards of space above the wall anyhow, the way Thornleigh's built these sheds for coolness. Let's see now, there's two saddles and four bridles. Take them across to the yard. I'll bring the pack saddles when I've got the guns from the car, if they're still there where that confounded black put them."

He helped Maddon get the saddles out of the door, crossing their stirrups over the seats to stop their clinking together. Then he went straight to the car shed and felt his way to the Minton. He opened the boot silently. . . . Good! His own rifle and shells were still there and Maddon's automatic and the calico bag he kept his bullets in, that Mason had found in the camp and handed to the blackfellow to put with the guns. Graster let down the boot door silently, moved out of the shed and closed the wide door.

But the feel of the rifle in his hands brought a new thought. He hesitated, his lips drawn back in a tigerish snarl.

At the horse yard he found Maddon had already bridled two horses and had a saddle on one.

"You won't want the pack saddles," he whispered

to Graster. "These are the only two horses in the yard." Graster set down the pack saddles with a grunt. He had half expected this. In fact they might have found only one horse, kept in the yard to run the rest in with next morning. He threw a saddle on the other animal and, his eyes now used to the starlight, he recognised it as Thornleigh's pacer

"I'll take this one," he told Maddon. He spoke with some satisfaction, though he did not explain it to Maddon. This mare of Thornleigh's had some blood in her. She would be hard to kill. If it came to a race with the police she'd leave that brute of Maddon's behind. But that would be Maddon's bad luck! He pointed northward.

"Lead your horse clear of the homestead and keep on leading him till I catch up with you. The dogs are 'way over at the blacks' quarters but don't make any noise all the same. I'll be after you in five minutes. I must have dropped a box of shells when I picked up the pack saddles. Here's your automatic." There was a tense note in his voice that made Maddon look hard at him but he had turned and walked away before the other could speak.

It took Graster less than two minutes to reach the tent, standing ghostly in the starlight, its sides rolled half up and the door flap standing wide. He glanced back towards the yard. The tethered mare hadn't whinnied after the other horse, thank goodness. He brought his rifle forward. . . . He could hear the steady breathing of the three exhausted men within. But, exhausted though they were, they would be no easy mark. No chance, in this light, of holding up all three, even if Maddon would have consented to help him. No chance to get the map now. If he shot them all there would be no time to search for it. But he'd never have a better chance to even scores with Mason; to kill him and get away without being seen. And leave Maddon to ride alone into a police trap. Maddon was a wanted man, had been wanted for a long time for a shooting, and he was helpless in this back country without a guide. The police would have him within forty-eight hours. He crouched and moved three steps closer. The rifle barrel glistened in the starlight. In the quietness he could distinguish each sleeper's quiet breathing.

But in that instant the stifling silence was torn asunder by a metallic clamour that seemed to leap out of the tent and fill the whole night! Graster jumped sideways and crouched in the shadow of the York gum. In the tent came a creaking and a loud thump and the fearful hammering stopped as suddenly as it had begun. Then Graster heard Blue's voice, extremely wide awake.

"Dogfoot! . . ."

But Geoff's voice cut in, laughing.

"Heck, I thought I was in that darned tunnel again and Graster was taking pot shots at me! Thanks a lot, Dogfoot!"

"Oh, thanks a lot!" Blue mocked. "Well, you've got your gun in your hand and it's pointing at me. What I'm suggesting is that you give it to Dogfoot to hop out round behind the York gum and do himself in with."

"Me no fixem that red feller sing out longa stomach ache, Boss! Me only windem! That one piccaninny blong Micky Tinker, 'im bin fool with 'im longa car shed. Might be that feller piccaninny bin fixem sing out longa stomach ache! Me bin tellem that one piccaninny. . . ."

"Okay, Dogfoot, Okay," Geoff laughed. The big hunter's apologies were getting more and more involved. "You bin lucky feller me no makem everybody full of daylight!" Still laughing, he looked down in some surprise at the automatic in his hand.

Five minutes later the tent was quiet again, the only sound the breathing of three sleeping men. But Graster could not hear it. Well beyond the homestead trees he swung into the saddle and joined Maddon. They rode away northward.

CHAPTER NINETEEN

DOGFOOT ASKS A QUESTION

When next Geoff woke it was to find Dick Thornleigh beside his bed. The tent was dark and stifling though the sides were still up. He sat up quickly.

"Why, Mr. Thornleigh . . ."

He glanced at his watch, surprised to find it was six o'clock but the tent was as dark as early dawn. Dogfoot stirred and lifted himself on an elbow, but Blue slept on.

"Good morning, Geoff," Thornleigh said, quietly. "There's a black dust-storm coming over and you'd better pin your tent down before it blows away. But that's not all I'm here to tell you, worse luck. Two of your men have got away—Graster and Maddon." He paused. "They burnt their ropes with a cigar butt—the saddle room reeks of stale cigar smoke still; and they've got away on the two horses that were in the yard for the night. Probably made their break pretty early, by ten o'clock, perhaps."

"A cigar!" Geoff said quietly. He recalled Monsieur missing his cigar last night. "Gone since ten o'clock, you think? Got a pretty good start again, haven't they? But there's no need to tell M'sieur—about the cigar, I mean, Mr. Thornleigh. He'd be broken up about it."

Thornleigh was silent for several seconds. Then

he laughed quietly and slapped Geoff's pyjama-clad shoulder.

"I was hoping you'd say that. Well, they've got a good start, as you say. Micky the Tinker was running late this morning and he didn't find the horses gone from the yard till half an hour ago. I'm afraid I have no suggestions to make but you won't do much tracking once this storm comes. Anyhow have a talk with Blue and let me know what you'd like to do and I'll help all I can. And now I'm afraid I'll have to go. This desert storm is going to make things a bit difficult with the stock. You'd better get your tent lashed, right away. Then if you think of anything, let me know."

An hour later the trio sat in a tent that cracked and banged like a live thing and ate breakfast by lantern light. Geoff and Blue discussed Graster's escape. In the end Geoff made his decision. He spoke quietly, but his eyes were narrowed. Blue had seen that look when his friend had leant over a charred map on a hotel balcony, a thousand miles east.

"It's like this Blue. You and Dogfoot came after me and got me out of bother and so far we're on the right side with the police. But my bit of fun at the gorge and bringing in those chaps tied up ready for the police was about as far as we can go. Now don't get me wrong. I'm not letting up on Graster. But I've done what I chiefly came out here for—to get evidence against him, or make him show his hand again. Now the police have taken him over, so to speak. They're chaps I've got a lot of time for. They won't chase everybody people want them to, but once they're convinced, they stay on a job—if it takes years. Probably the smartest thing we can do now is to keep out of their way. Anyhow, one thing, we'd better be clear about is that we've got no legal right to go chasing Graster and Maddon. If we do and there's more gun play, the plain fact is a lawyer could put us behind bars along with them."

Blue nodded.

"'Fraid you're right, me boy. So what?"

"Well, those jokers will get a long way in this dust-storm and I think they'll light out for the north. But the police are taking a hand now, as I said." He stood up and the anger left his eyes as he laughed. "The best thing we can do for the present is get on with our search for that ridge of Uncle George's. We might find out what happened there; and we might find what opals he left. But I reckon we can do something to help Thornleigh, first."

The tent swayed wildly, then cracked like a pistol shot. Blue looked up gloomily at the tossing roof of it.

"Time to take in stuns'ls and royals, I'd say," he remarked casually. "Also, there's sand in the sardines."

Geoff grinned then raised his voice in the increasing din.

"This red-hot storm will mean that the cattle will want more water, and it'll give them farther to travel to the wells because the wind will burn off the badly punished saltbush nearest the bores."

And when presently they walked across to the car shed they found Thornleigh and two native stockmen loading a four-hundred gallon tank on the station truck. It seemed he intended to set up canvas troughs ten miles from the bores and cart water to them.

"We can't hope to water two thousand head, of course, but we can take care of some of the yearling stock."

"Any chance of borrowing a truck from another station, Mr. Thornleigh?"

"Well as a matter of fact Matthews rang up to tell me his is there but he can't start it. Right Jimmy!" to one of the black stockmen who climbed into the truck and drove away. "The other chaps are a good way away and all of us manage with one truck each, which means we've always got plenty of use for them. Matthews also offered to take some of my cattle on to his bores but he's got himself over-stocked and it would only make more trouble if I accepted his offer."

"Well, there's Graster's utility. It'll take a small tank—say two hundred gallons," Geoff said.

"And how about if I take a run over and look at that non-starter of Mr. Matthews?" Blue asked. Thornleigh laughed.

"You boys certainly know how to help!"

The result of that conversation was that within two hours two trucks and the utility were crossing and recrossing the eaten-out northern side of Matoorlie, toiling steadily southward with water sloshing in the tanks and pouring it into canvas troughs, then rumbling back to the bores for more. Geoff drove the utility and Blue the truck from Matthews' station. The stockmen and Dogfoot rode a line to the southward, letting the young cattle in to the troughs and driving them back again and forcing the cows away altogether so that they had to use the bores. But by the end of the second day it was clear the whites and hard-riding stockmen were fighting a losing fight. During that night almost every hoof of the place had moved in to the bores and refused to budge next morning. Over six hundred had already been on the water for two days without a mouthful of fodder. All hands set to work to drive the poor bellowing brutes to graze, and it was clear enough to all that very little more of such treatment would result in heavy losses. Indeed eight bullocks were already lying dead near Number 3 bore.

On the third night the fiery wind dropped. But that afternoon Thornleigh's weary horse fell and threw him heavily, jerking a muscle in his back so badly that he had to be lifted into a truck and driven home. Geoff was more than a little touched at the look of genuine concern on the faces of the two stockmen who helped to lift the cattle-man.

"Me wantem Big Boss ride horse blonga me," Micky the Tinker said ruefully to Geoff as Blue drove off. All the stockmen called Thornleigh the "Big Boss" to distinguish him from Fawkner the overseer.

That night, in the tent, Dogfoot asked a question.

"What for Big Boss no makem bore longa topside?"

"He means the south side," Blue explained to Geoff. Then, to Dogfoot. "Him silly fellow makem bore that way. No water longa topside."

Dogfoot looked at them for a moment, then spoke quietly.

"That one ridge me findem piccaninny dingo—Big Boss makem bore there, 'im findem plenty water."

The big black rose and strolled to the tent opening, his bare feet noiseless on the clean-swept canvas spread for a floor. Geoff watched him stooping a little to roll a cigarette. The beggar strolled off as if there was nothing more to be said! He seemed to have merely stated a fact, not expressed an opinion! He looked wonderingly at Blue. The latter merely shrugged.

The sun was just rising next morning when the three friends stood on a limestone ridge top. It was the ridge on which Dogfoot had caught the dingo cub. The black stood still now, and pointed a long finger downwards.

"Water 'im bin longa this one place."

Again he spoke as one stating a fact; indeed there was faint surprise in his voice as though he failed to understand why they should hesitate to agree with him. Geoff looked from his face to the rock at his feet. Dogfoot was telling them that there was water under these durn-awful barren ridges! Pointing almost as though he were pointing *at* it! He remembered the big black's sudden rigid stance that afternoon after he'd picked up the dingo cub.

Geoff looked at Blue's poker face. They were prize idiots to come all this way this morning! He'd heard stories of blacks' uncanny ability to find water, but they concerned surface water, not sub-artesian. He turned and strode ten yards due north across the ridge.

"You come longa me now, Dogfoot."

The black seemed to hesitate, then started towards Geoff, his bare feet slapping faintly on the smooth limestone. But before he got half-way he halted, calmly returned to the spot he had left and stood pointing downwards!

Five minutes later Geoff straightened from setting a last stone on a little pile of conglomerate on the ridge top. Then he led the way to the Minton. Neither he nor Blue said anything till the latter had snaked the car over the mile of ridge and valley to the plain. When the big sports was purring along the station track Geoff glanced at his friend.

"What do you think?"

Blue shook his head.

"Not the slightest use asking me, feller. Seems pretty potty to me drilling for water on the top of a ridge, for a start. On the other hand, what about these chaps with divining rods?"

It was Geoff's turn to shake his head.

"Some chaps who practise divining are frauds. Others really believe in it. As far as I know it's been neither proved nor disproved but none of the big shows seem to bother with it. Anyhow this little joke is for Thornleigh to decide. Matthews' truck has to go back to-morrow and the utility's just about had it. But, even now the wind's dropped, Thornleigh will have to keep on carting all the water he can and if we get another three-day desert wind, which is more that probable . . ."

They were back and had had breakfast by the time

Monsieur, his own breakfast over, strolled into the summer-house. Monsieur had constituted himself medical adviser (and practitioner) for Thornleigh now, as well as Lakker. The latter's spear wound was healing only slowly and he still could not walk. Geoff had had a long telephone conversation with Calwell at Burramoola and he was satisfied the police were spreading a net for Graster and Maddon that would give the scoundrels a good deal of worry. He was satisfied, too, that the plan was better than trying to track them, now the hot desert wind-storms seemed to have started. As for Lakker, Thornleigh had consented to let the little man stay till he could walk, when the police would come and get him.

Monsieur waved to Blue and Geoff as they approached the summer-house. "Deeck, 'e not ver' good," he said sorrowfully in answer to their inquiry as they walked quietly up the steps. They found Thornleigh propped on a settee and sat down near him in deck chairs. But when it came to broaching the matter of Dogfoot's "divining," Geoff found himself more than a little shamefaced. But Thornleigh heard him out without a word. Then he looked past them both through the home-stead trees at the dusty bare plain round the nearest bore. He turned back with a sigh.

"As you say, Geoff, there's probably nothing in it at all. I'm no more a believer in divining than yourself. But I'm up against it, as you can see." Suddenly he was chuckling quietly. "A drowning man clutching at a straw doesn't fit my case considering the trouble is shortage of water. But you're offering to take my boring plant across there and bump down a hole. I'll be very grateful if you'll go ahead, boys, very glad. There's no one to help you till I can get round again, though, and I must confess I know little enough about the business. Jim Fawkner was my man on the boring and he was no expert as he was ready enough to admit. But. . . ."

"Well, that's fine, Mr. Thornleigh. I've had a good look at your plant and it's in first-rate order. Been taken proper care of."

He stood up as Barbara and Madame came out of the house.

"Goodness, Madame, this looks like a council of war," Barbara laughed. Blue picked up his hat.

"We're just going to punch a hole in this station's hardest and horniest corner. We like it tough! That's the sort of chaps we are. So, if that devil or whatever it is laughs at us . . ."

"Ugh!" Barbara exclaimed, her face suddenly serious. "I hope you don't hear that awful thing again. It sounded like a . . . like a madman!"

Geoff chuckled. "He'll have nothing on us, then, I reckon, because we're going to drill in about the most unlikely spot known to man. However, here we go! So long everybody."

CHAPTER TWENTY

SLAVES OF THE LAMP

THE BIG chisel's clanking rang clear in the early morning air—clank clank, clank clank, at two-second intervals, on and on, far across the desolation of the ridges. Blue looked at the tall drilling tower and then at its long shadow, flung far down the smooth slope of limestone, then at the sun, just clear of the horizon, its brassy gold turned reddish by dust haze.

"Drought'll be on all day to-day," he told Geoff solemnly as the latter stood, one eye closed, checking the rise and fall of the eight-foot drill stem on its steel cable. "And at the end of the day this hole will be a foot deeper! . . . Four days, four feet! How deep do we go for this artesian water, feller?"

Geoff grinned, but without interrupting his watch on the clanking drill stem.

"We're not boring for artesian water. You go down half a mile or more for that and, when you get it, it spouts up the shaft and out, to the tune of, perhaps half a million gallons a day. But what we're after is sub-artesian water, which we might get at any depth between two hundred and five hundred feet. But if we do find it we'll have to pump it up, and we'll be lucky if we get twenty thousand gallons a day. Now is that clear? If not I'll say it again."

But Blue's gloom seemed to deepen as he moved round to the clutch lever.

"Artesian water, half a mile deep, spouts up; sub-artesian, 500 feet, prefers to be pumped up. Well, I'll settle for sub-artesian. At our present rate of progress, working week-ends, we should get to it, if it's there, in a little over a year from now."

At a signal from Geoff he threw the clutch. The clanking stopped and he started the cable drum. It wound the cable the few feet to withdraw the drill stem from the shaft. Geoff drew it towards him as it swung, suspended at eye level, and examined the drill point. The hour's work had blunted and burred it badly. He shook his head as he took the big spanner Blue handed him and began removing the drill point from the stem to fit a sharp one.

"I've struck some hard rock before but this stuff seems almost harder than granite—as hard as a blessed diamond!"

He glanced at the sky. The dust was thickening rapidly in the west and the sky was turning greyish. Blue looked at it too, but this time he made no comment. Though grumbling was his way of facing unpleasant possibilities, having done that, he was never afraid to meet what came. Dogfoot, his khaki shirt draped like a smock over his shorts, was stooping above a small fire well away from the several drums of crude oil for the diesel engine. Farther away still, down in the little valley, the Minton glinted in the sickly sunlight. He straightened and called that breakfast was ready.

"Okay, feller," Geoff said to Blue. Blue waited till the drill stem was once more in the short shaft and bumping again, then went across and sat down on a bag Dogfoot had spread on the rock surface. As he ate he surveyed several crooked tree branches lying tumbled on the limestone. He and Dogfoot proposed to rig a tent to-day as a protection for provisions. That had been Barbara's suggestion when she and Monsieur had driven up yesterday. But it mightn't be worth while putting it up to-day after all, Blue thought, with heavy wind coming, for there was no easy way of anchoring the tent poles in the rock. A storm would blow the tent away, poles and all.

He decided against erecting the tent and he had reason to be glad, for long before noon the storm was upon them. They kept the drill going, though for an hour there was scarcely daylight enough to move round by. When the first black dusty cloud passed the gale seemed to grow hotter and hotter, for the sun's heat was increasing hour by hour. By mid-afternoon even Dogfoot was panting as he moved about the clanking drill and the hot diesel, in a sun temperature that was round 160 degrees.

"Cæsar," Geoff gasped. "With this wind and the sun cracking down on you and the heat coming up again from the rock—phew! Anyhow, here we go with another drill."

With Blue at the clutch, he guided the chisel into the shaft with its sixth new drill for the day and the clanking began once more. Blue left the droning diesel and came and stood beside him. Geoff lugged his hat tighter on his head and turned a shoulder to the wind. He looked north-eastward across the saltbush plain. This storm showed every sign of being worse than the last one, and Thornleigh had only one truck for the water carting. To-morrow he and Blue had better give the stockmen a hand again. Eighteen bullocks, altogether, had died after the last gruelling dust-storm, but it began to look as though that was only a beginning. There'd be more dead stock after this dust-storm. And Thornleigh had told him every station within two hundred miles was too well stocked up to take any cattle on agistment. That meant he had to hang on without help till rain came. But half a dozen more of these fire-hot storms would beat Thornleigh. In other words, with thousands of acres of untouched saltbush at his back, the cattleman was headed for a financial crash. His thirsty cattle just couldn't get out to the saltbush that grew high and thick on this south side of the big run.

Geoff reached out, twisted the drill stem as it bumped, and looked at Blue standing opposite him. Blue was watching the cable as it see-sawed on the pulley in the top of the tower. Geoff glanced down at the six-inch shaft with the drill stem rising and falling in it . . . and suddenly tensed! From the edge of the round shaft, the edge nearest to Blue, a crack had started! It was six inches long when he saw it and it seemed alive, for it lengthened two feet while he stared, the ends of it darting to and fro like a snake, towards Blue's boots. Then it turned sharply to the right, seeming to whip across the limestone. But now another crack darted from his own side of the shaft, darting out from it and snaking out and round to meet the other! Geoff sprang across past the shaft and was pointing down as he grasped Blue's arm.

"Look!"

The ends of both cracks turned towards each other, moving in little darts, right and left. Then, a foot apart, they seemed to pause. Next instant they flashed forward and met!

There came a grinding, tearing sound, merged with a low roar. Then the two boys saw that the rock surface encircled by the crack was sinking! Sinking slowly, a quarter-inch, half an inch, leaving jagged edges showing stark in the sunlight.

And then suddenly, there was no rock, but a six-foot-wide jagged hole, filled with rushing water and with steam; water that spurted in a great jet slantwise out of the wide, gaping hole, spurted twenty feet in the air, arched and clattered on the hot limestone in the hot sunlight! It sped away down the south slope of the fire-hot ridge in a spreading stream twenty feet wide, the wide front edge like a spent breaker on the sand, frothy and stained with reddish dust. The wind slashed at the glittering surface of it, but it rushed on unheeding, down the ridge and into the valley floor. As Blue staggered back and threw the clutch he saw a creaming head of water swill round the tyres of the Minton!

It was minutes before the two could speak coherently! In that time they had slapped Dogfoot on the back, shaken hands, laughed, and laughed again, shaken hands again and once again thumped

Dogfoot's broad shoulders and each other's, and when they found the water was not hot enough to scald, they stood where it splashed, first round their legs and then their bodies.

At last Blue pointed down the little valley that swung away to the right.

"Look at it racing down the valley! Well, what are we waiting for? We'd better let 'em know at the homestead!" He had almost to shout above the noise.

"Sure," Geoff laughed. "But—just one minute."

The drill plant's diesel was still idling, its fly-wheel spinning smoothly. His eyes sparkling with excitement Geoff released the brake of the cable slowly. The eight-foot drill stem was already half hidden in the steamy darkness of the yawning hole from which came a steady humming sound. With the easing of its cable, it descended slowly, clearing the great water jet by quite two feet, till the top of its shank disappeared. Still the drum revolved slowly, paying out the steel cable; but, within ten seconds, Geoff felt the strain of the stem's weight go off the drum. The drill had touched bottom. But, from the stains on the cable itself, Geoff had been able to make a rough check of the length paid out. He shouted at Blue, his excitement almost mastering him again.

"About twenty feet to the bottom. We've busted into some sort of cavity twenty feet deep." The drill stem shot up into view as he reversed the drum and then he braked the drum and stopped the engine. He turned and still laughing, thumped his friend's wet shoulder again.

"Boy, oh boy! Two hundred thousand gallons a day or I'll eat my head! Let's go!" He snatched up a billy can, held its lip to the tumbling water till it was full, then jogged after Blue and Dogfoot slopping their way through the inch-deep stream that raced under the Minton.

The English lad started the car. The little valley in which it stood was curved and ended in a cul-de-sac, as so many of these strange, twisted valleys did. At its end they found a shallow pool already fifty feet long and half as wide, its surface catspawed and rippled by the swishing wind gusts. They gazed in amazement. Half an hour ago that valley end was baking hot in the sun. This pool seemed to have been *put* there; spirited there from another world!

Blue swung away to the left and presently they were on the saltbush and speeding across the station. Geoff glanced back once at Dogfoot, towering in the dicky seat of the big sports. The hunter grinned at him, obviously pleased that they were pleased, yet he had not joined in their wild excitement. Half-way to the homestead they could see a wind-whipped dust-cloud to the right, where Thornleigh's stockmen were battling with the cattle.

Blue drove to the tent, for their clothes were still damp. All three made a high speed change, then Geoff took Dogfoot by the elbow.

"You're in on this, feller," he laughed, forgetting to talk pidgin. Then the trio strode together across to the side gate of the garden, Geoff carrying the billy-can, still three parts full.

Apparently the noise of the wind had prevented

anyone hearing the car drive up, for the men were all away and the house lubras were shut indoors from the gale. The blinds were down along the western wall of the summer-house. The three reached it unheralded. Geoff set the billy on the ground as Barbara got up from a chair near her father's settee.

"Why, Geoff—is something wrong? Why, come in, all of you!" She stopped and looked over quickly as her mother came from the house, Monsieur behind her. Madame sat still in a deck chair and fanned herself vigorously, for the air, out of the gale, was stifling. Then Thornleigh spoke. If he was surprised at seeing all three of them together he did not show it, for as usual his voice was quiet and steady.

"Struck trouble, boys? I was afraid you would, with that diamond-hard limestone."

There was a moment's silence before Geoff answered. He forced the exultation from his voice.

"No, Mr. Thornleigh. We've got better news than that. We've struck water."

He watched amazement come slowly into the cattle-man's face. Thornleigh's hand reached out and gripped the table by his bed.

"Water!"

Now the sick man was struggling to raise himself. Monsieur stepped forward and thrust an arm under his shoulders and helped him to a sitting position.

"Artesian water, Mr. Thornleigh."

"Artesian! . . ." Thornleigh paused, then laughed. "You're not serious, of course! But . . ."

"It's artesian water, Mr. Thornleigh, and a terrific flow of it! Don't ask me how it's happened. We seem to have knocked in the roof of a cave, or something, and right on top of a fissure that's letting the water up!" He turned to Dogfoot.

"Fetchem that one billy can, Dogfoot." Then to Thornleigh again, "Tasted all right to me, Mr. Thornleigh." The big black was back in an instant with the can. Thornleigh took it as one in a dream, tasted the water and set the can on the floor. He spoke almost in a whisper now.

"But . . . but boys, this is stupendous news! First quality, sweet water! . . . A . . . a big flow you say?"

"About two hundred thousand gallons a day, I'd reckon. It'll about half fill that little valley that curls into a dead end just east of where we drove the shaft—and keep it half full, cracks, evaporation and all!"

As though they had rehearsed a sort of unison speech, Madame, Barbara, Mrs. Thornleigh and Monsieur all exclaimed together, but Barbara and her mother were no match for their excitable guests and the latter resorted, as usual, to laughing. At last, however, she took a long breath.

"Oh Daddy! Mummy! Oh *dear*! . . . What are we waiting here for?"

The Packard and Thornleigh's car made a swift journey across the station, Geoff driving Thornleigh's car, the injured cattle-man propped in the back seat, his wife beside him. As the two cars approached the south-east corner, something flashed and flashed on a ridge top two miles away.

"There's your bore, Mr. Thornleigh."

The cattle-man stared as if he doubted his senses and the others with him. As the car rapidly shortened the distance they could see the vast jet of water arching in the sunlight. Then they turned in off the saltbush and within five minutes both cars were drawn up on a ridge top. Below them the little valley was already a lagoon. Blue and Madame and Monsieur got out while the others gazed, and came to their car, Madame already launched into rapid French, to which Monsieur replied, also at a high speed. When they paused for a moment, Barbara drew another long breath.

"But . . . Oh Daddy, it can't be but it *is*!"

She joined in the shout of laughter.

Thornleigh's face showed only sheer amazement. In the midst of the exclamations and laughter he said nothing at all; but presently he touched Geoff's arm and they drove to the bore itself. There followed an hour of questions, speculations and more exclamations, till the sun was almost down. With the noise of the water demanding that everyone shout, conversation became so strenuous that Geoff started the car again and moved it a short distance from the bore.

"How on *earth* could Dogfoot have known it was here?" Barbara demanded. "Just exactly at this spot?"

"I've been wondering that too," Geoff said. "But I think I've got an idea—simply that he *felt* it, felt the vibration of the water pounding up under that cavern roof. He comes along barefooted and stands exactly above where that darned great jet was striking the rock. As a matter of fact he seemed surprised that Blue and I couldn't feel it, but he didn't say so. I suppose 'vibration' isn't a word he could think up the pidgin English for."

Barbara laughed.

"Bright boy! Go to the top of your class!"

"But the water—it spurts out of a fissure about twenty feet below the limestone 'roof,' you think, Geoff," Thornleigh asked.

"I think so, Mr. Thornleigh. Some of the oases in the Sahara seemed to have been formed centuries ago by a set-up like that; and it's pretty obvious this terrific pressure head has been wearing the 'roof' away from below. Hot water pounding at limestone like that would both wear it away and dissolve it, I should imagine. Don't you think so, M'sieur?"

But for perhaps the twentieth time, Monsieur was on his way from the car back to the water jet. He stopped for the twentieth time over the jagged hole filled with its vapour and the strangely even humming sound. He peered into the blackness for perhaps ten seconds, then he straightened and came back to them again, shaking his head vigorously.

"Deeck," he said, and his face seemed full of foreboding. "Ze black 'ole, I do not like 'im, *non*! Undoubtedly 'e is ze 'ome of ze devil!"

But Thornleigh slipped his arm round his wife's shoulders. She smiled up at him and then they both gazed once more at the great pressure head tossing down its tumbling water with never an instant's pause. They gazed as though, even yet, they could not believe their eyes.

"Thousands of gallons an hour, Helen!" the big man said softly. "And four hours ago we were facing ruin!"

CHAPTER TWENTY-ONE

LAKKER TALKS

Two days later Geoff and Blue sat their horses and watched a hundred bellowing cows trotting eagerly down the ridge slope that formed the eastern bank of a lagoon whose water lapped at no reed-grown margin but on hot, bare rock. Lower down the slope Dogfoot and Micky the Tinker waited, well-mounted and swinging their heavy whips to steady the thirsty cattle and make them spread out round the water's edge. The hot wind had dropped suddenly, an hour ago.

"Well, that's the last of them, poor beggars," Geoff said. "Now, every hoof on the station is up in this corner and there's enough fodder in this corner alone to last them a year. Well, thank goodness this flat country's dead easy to muster. Even so, it's been a hot enough job shifting two thousand head thirty miles."

Blue nodded.

"The blighters fought us every foot," he growled. "Wouldn't believe a word I told 'em about this lagoon till they got near enough to smell it for themselves."

He and Geoff had been two days in the saddle, lending a hand to move the cattle to the new water. It had meant hard riding for, as Blue said, the cattle had fought back towards the only water they knew about—the bores on the northern side.

"And Thornleigh says he can run the water north-east from here in a drain," Blue continued.

"That's right," Geoff answered. "The country slopes that way. The sandy patches will take it up like a sieve for a while but he'll run it five miles and perhaps ten I reckon. Anyhow he intends eventually to case the jet and pipe the water clear of the ridges and later on, when he can afford to, he reckons to pipe it across the run. Jove, has this business bucked him up! And M'sieur's so pleased about it he's taken to talking it over in French with Lakker. And the funny thing is Lakker seems as pleased as anybody. Another funny thing. It seems Thornleigh and M'sieur and Lakker were all in that red-hot show at Bullecourt in the old War. Their battalion went in nine hundred strong and only about 250 of them came out. Lakker was there all right. He answered all M'sieur's questions and now both M'sieur and Thornleigh have placed him."

Blue nodded, his face full of interest.

"Lord, those old Somme battles must have been a blood bath! Here, hold up, now!"

The last remark was to his horse which had reefed at the bit in a bid to follow the cattle down to the water. Geoff twisted in the saddle and pointed along the ridge to the tall drill derrick against the sky. The settling sun flashed on the pressure head of the artesian flow.

"There she is, still pelting it out! And she'll do that twenty-four hours a day, probably for ever. But that brings me to something feller. Thornleigh, as I said, thinks he could case the jet and pipe it clear of the ridges. That'll save pumping from the lagoon because he's doubtful if syphoning will work satisfactorily. So am I. Anyhow I think he'd like to know just what's down under there so as to make arrangements about the casing job, if it's possible. He didn't say so, of course. But I was looking at that hole this morning. You could get down into it right under the drill drop and have a look at the fissure that's letting the water up. I took a torch with me but the vapour's like a fog—can't see a yard into it. And yet, all you'd have to do would be to put a ladder over the edge and climb down."

Blue eyed him gloomily.

"Yes," he assented. "Should be interesting too—hot water, steam and carbon dioxide to breathe and plenty of nice cracks to fall down. Also, there should be a devil or two. Well, I suppose I'd better come with you and see you don't get into more bother. But I reckon the next job had better be getting that boring plant back under cover after what some of those gusts did to her."

"That's so," Geoff answered. "There's no chance to anchor her properly without blasting a few holes in the rock and the wind's likely to get up again any time. We could just dismantle her of course, but it won't take much longer to pack her up and take her home." He tightened his bridle reins. "So you're coming underground with me. Darned glad to have you, feller, though it's my own fool idea and there's no reason why you should. Incidentally, they haven't passed the word round yet about this water. Thornleigh couldn't entertain visitors while he had his cattle to shift. So now I'll get him to wait another day or two till we've shifted the plant home and done a spot of exploring. Well, we'd better give the horses a drink and start for home ourselves. We've got a long ride." He wheeled to lead the way down amongst the cows and the water, but reined up quickly.

"Hullo, here comes Barbara!"

They both swung their horses and rode along the ridge to meet the girl driving her father's car towards them. She laughed up at them from beside Monsieur.

"Daddy says you're to leave your horses for Micky the Tinker. I'm sorry to be spoiling you, but orders are orders."

Dogfoot elected to help Micky the Tinker move the cows back and then ride home with him, leading the other horses. The English boy climbed stiffly into the back seat with Geoff. The two gruelling days in the saddle with the fiery desert wind swirling dust and sand, had been no picnic.

"Now I can ache in comfort," he mentioned gloomily and lowered himself tenderly on to the cushion.

That night, perhaps because he and Lakker had fought some battles over again, insomnia attacked Monsieur and at 3 a.m. he gave up the fight and adjourned to the summer-house for a smoke. Whereupon sleep assailed him, he slumped in his chair and his cigar rolled away and set fire to a canvas blind. Lakker, however, had also been wakeful. He saw the blaze, hobbled to the garden and turned on the hose before he thought to give the alarm. After which he put out the fire and, not being quite sure, because of the smoke, whether or not Monsieur was also burning, hosed him through the side door of the summer-house and down the steps.

"Well," Blue remarked, an hour later, as he sat on his bed, "I was stiff and sore, but I wouldn't have missed hearing M'sieur cuss Lakker in French, Italian and Esperanto for all the sleep there is! And all done in between swallows of water!"

Geoff chuckled from his pillow. Then he raised himself on his elbow.

"Now we're on the subject of Lakker, Blue, I've been wondering if that little joker's . . . well . . . if he's worth giving a chance. What do you reckon? It's my bet he's been in trouble and Graster's had some sort of hold over him. That's the way hounds like Graster work. Anyhow, from what I've seen of Lakker, I'm beginning to think he wasn't directly concerned with Uncle George's death. I was going to leave it to the police to question him; but, now, instead, I think it might be an idea to give him a chance to tell his story and, if we're satisfied I'm pretty certain the police will be."

Blue didn't answer for several seconds, but sat looking through the tent door at the paling sky.

"But Lakker was waiting at the gorge with a gun," he said at last.

"He *had* a gun. But you can have a gun and do a lot of missing."

"You *can*! *I* can. But, look here, you'd think you were the beggar's lawyer to hear you talk! All the same . . . well, I can judge a man pretty well myself and I think you might have the right idea. However, as it's four ak emma, I move the house adjourn."

After breakfast the following morning the two friends found Lakker hobbling round in his sleeping quarters. As they entered he had just finished making his bed. The little man had seen Geoff come from the house and had assumed that he had been to the 'phone to make arrangements for sending him to Burramoola and had come with Blue to inform him. There was little but hopelessness in his face as he sat on his bed and looked up at them. But long before Geoff had finished speaking his list-lessness was gone and his eyes were eager and, when he answered, his voice shook with eagerness. He had jerked himself to his feet and stood, one hand on a small table.

"It was Don Graster. All my trouble come from that devil Graster—all the worst of it, anyhow. He found me out in some business . . . well, I'm not denyin' I was a fool and I was on the wrong side o' the law. But I'd squared things up in me own way. And then I was fool enough to let that devil scare me; and now, instead of bein' liable for three months' gaol like I was when he found me out, I'm up for years—perhaps ten year! An' he's worked me like a nigger, runnin' his messages an' taking his orders. But as for doin' his killin', no! . . . You seen me with a gun at the gorge. But you needn't have worried, boys. Not one o' my bullets would've gone within a yard of y'. Dirk Maddon . . . well, Graster knows a lot more about 'im than I do. But

I will say this. Maddon's town bred. He don't know how to get *out* o' this country. If he did there'd be a show-down between them two."

"What happened the night my uncle's farm was burnt?"

Lakker sat down on his bed again, then looked up and ran the tip of his tongue over his lips.

"I thought we was headin' for that." He paused as though marshalling his words, then looked Geoff squarely in the face. "I was outside, on watch, Mister Geoff, an' most of what I know is from what Maddon said. That's not evidence." There was a set to the little man's jaw.

"Okay," Geoff said quietly. "You mean you're not prepared to squeal. Go on."

"Well, it seems like Maddon pulled 'is gun on your uncle and then Graster hit him hard, twice, with 'is gun butt an' set to work to Third Degree 'im. In the end, your uncle told them there was a map in a deed box in the writing desk. Graster 'ad just found the box, it seems, when I seen your car stop at the gate in the road an' I run in to warn 'em. Your uncle had sort of come round a bit an' was tryin' to get up, Maddon said, but Graster hit him hard again and he crumpled up against the wall. The lamp got knocked over and oil flew everywhere and flared. That was the way it was when I got there. I started to drag your uncle out when Graster lashed out and kicked me in the stomach an' the next I knew the two of 'em was dragging me along between 'em. You muster just missed spottin' us getting away amongst the sheds. Anyway, while you was in the house we got clear away and down to the truck we'd hid in the trees beside the road."

He paused. The three could hear, faintly, the voices of lubras over at the house and a crow cawing down towards No. 3 Bore. Blue could see the veins stand out on Geoff's neck and knew his friend was fighting back his anger. At last Geoff spoke.

"One more question, Lakker. How did Graster get to know my uncle had made an opal find?"

But Lakker shook his head.

"I just don't know, Mister Geoff. 'E mighter told Dirk but they kept it from me. What's more, I didn't know what you told Graster in the camp—about 'im desertin' your uncle out beyond 'ere."

Geoff stood looking down at him in silence. The little man had spoken simply, without trying to whine his way out. Moreover, there was no doubt that his story tallied up. And there was no doubt that Graster and Maddon between them had killed poor, warm-hearted old Uncle George . . . the cruel swine! . . . Again he fought back his fierce anger. Well, if Blue was satisfied. He looked at his friend, standing beside him. Blue met his glance and nodded. Geoff hesitated a moment longer, then spoke slowly.

"Okay, Lakker, we're satisfied. If the police collect Graster, you might be up for those three months you mentioned, but, since you say you've already squared things up, it's my bet the police will be willing to let the gruelling Graster's given you and this spear wound make up a pay-off. Apart from that, and as far as we're concerned, that's all. Mr. Thornleigh told me to tell you he's prepared to put you on his pay-roll as station gardener. However, that's up to yourself."

For the second time Lakker came to his feet, his face alight.

"Gee, Mister Geoff . . .!"

Geoff and Blue were moving to leave. But a vast figure suddenly filled the doorway. Lakker was laughing now, with tears streaming down his cheeks.

"M'sieur!—Gee, M'sieur, I got good news. Mister Geoff and Mister Blue, they're givin' me a break! An' Mister Thornleigh's given me a job. I'm station gardener!"

But, for once, Monsieur did not share the joy of a fellow creature. He was fingering his neck and he looked at Lakker sternly.

"Then, *mon ami*, will you please to remember ze 'ose is for gardens and not for ze 'uman? When at last I go to bed I dream I am ze tadpole an' yet my gill 'e do not work! *Non!*"

CHAPTER TWENTY-TWO

THE CAVE

"M'SIEUR GEOFF, I say it for ze 'undred time—it is ze place of *diables*!—— To 'ear 'im in ze dusk that is bad. But to climb into ze 'ole, *mon Dieu*, that is to meet 'im in ze darkness!"

Monsieur spoke earnestly, leaning forward in the car seat beside Thornleigh. Barbara, in the front seat, twisted to look back at him, then glanced at Geoff beside her.

"I think it's dangerous, too, M'sieur. For one thing that artesian water is giving off fumes and they must have been accumulating under there since goodness knows when. Then there's all that steam from it and there must be cracks and holes and the rock would be wet and slippery and it would be terribly dark and——" She was interrupted by delighted laughter from the boys.

"Now look here, Barbara," Geoff said at last, as he drove. "Take the fumes first. People are often deceived by the whiff of sulphuretted hydrogen they get from an artesian bore, but there's never much of it really. There'll be carbon dioxide, of course, but we can check on that by lowering a lantern first."

"And suppose the lantern causes an explosion?" Barbara demanded. Thornleigh chuckled.

"No risk of that in limestone, I think," he said.

"If it's near coal or oil you usually get explosive gas. Isn't that right, Geoff?"

"Yes. And, speaking of coal, any of you chaps ever been down a coal-mine? Now, if it's bother you want, a coal-mine provides plenty. A chap took me down an Illawarra mine, once, for a whole day. It happened to be a deep mine—a thousand feet. Well, they talk in miles, down there; in fact, we actually walked eleven miles altogether. But what interested me most was this. Near the coal faces the miners were actually hewing from, there were little pools of water; and every darned pool was covered with little breaking bubbles, just like the ones lemonade gives off when it's just poured. That was carbon dioxide coming out of the floor. That is to say, every square yard of the walls and floor of every tunnel and working was pushing out CO_2 at that speed. Yet, wherever we tramped, the air was fresh and moving and most of the time I could actually feel it on my face or the back of my neck. All right. There were those miles of tunnels all giving off CO_2 like the very dickens, yet the air was fresh! Thirty miles of tunnels, they told me. And that ventilation job was done by one big rotary fan drawing the air out of one shaft so that fresh air was drawn down another. Well, my idea is that that water jet is acting pretty much like a fan and it's already had a few days to ventilate that black hole of ours."

"But the steam, Geoff?" Barbara persisted.

"It's not steam really, Barbara. The temperature of the water's only 120°—hot, but a long way from boiling point. That 'steam' is just water vapour—fog. It stifles a torch beam and the sun-light but it will probably be quite easy to breathe in it."

The whole of the previous day had been given over to dismantling the plant and taking it back to the homestead and this was the fourth day since they had struck the water flow. The morning had been spent making ready such gear as they needed. Then they had all had an early lunch and come on up to the bore, Blue and Dogfoot in Thornleigh's truck.

Half an hour later the whole party stood in the red heat-shimmer on the ridge top and watched intently while Geoff hauled on a rope that disappeared into the hole at the end where the drill shaft had been. He lay flat on the hot rock surface, his head some two feet from the hissing jet. The rope came up yard by yard and Blue could see it was dry. Then Geoff got to his knees and out of the steamy darkness, came an ordinary hurricane lantern, its flame a pale yellow in the sunlight but burning clearly. Geoff met the gaze of his friends.

"It was down there three minutes—long enough to blacken some of the glass chimney if it had been smoking. But there's not a smear on the glass." He ran his finger over the metal base and frame of the lantern. There was no more than a suggestion of moisture on them.

"Well, so much for your steam clouds, Barbara. And that's about all we want to know now. Let's have the ladder, Blue."

With Dogfoot's help, they lowered a twenty-five foot ladder carefully between the rock lip and the gigantic water jet. It had to be done carefully for they knew the water could jerk it from their hands. When they felt it find firm support below, Blue spoke to Dogfoot.

"You holdem tight longa top end."

Thornleigh had insisted that the first man to go down should do so with a rope round him just in case he should be overcome by fumes. Geoff picked up the rope and tied one end securely under his arms. He grinned at Blue.

"One at a time, feller. And I thought of it first." Without more ado he clambered onto the ladder and began at once to move down, rung by rung, keeping just clear of the hissing water. Presently only his head was out of the hole, the vapour curling across his face, the steady humming all round him. Then he grinned up at Barbara's strained face and disappeared into the vapour cloud.

With the sunlight cut off, he flashed on his torch. Its rays made a yellow halo a foot from its glass, but that was all. He felt the heat was increasing but his breathing was unaffected by the vapour. He stepped down another rung and yet another till his shoulders were below the under surface of the five-foot thickness of rock that formed the cavern's roof. Still he had no difficulty as to breathing, nor was the noise of the water greater. Then he stepped down to the next rung.

On the instant, in place of the subdued humming, a thunderous roar filled his ears. It was like the roar of a fast train coursing across a steel bridge. The suddenness of it deafened and almost unnerved him, and he had to fight back an impulse to scramble up again. Then he gripped the ladder rungs tighter and moved down step by step.

But now he found his torch ray stabbed out quite three yards into the blackness. That meant the warm vapour was rising, was thicker at the top of the hole or up under the roof. He kept the torch beam directed downwards now—and saw the rock floor at last.

In five seconds more, his ears drumming to the pent-up din of the water, he was standing on almost level rock apparently red sandstone. Three feet away, two water jets sprang out of it—the giant one roared up past his head at an angle of 75° and out through what looked from below like a black cloud; the other, a small one, arching away to his right, its water apparently striking the floor of the cavern somewhere out in the darkness.

He put his hand to the rope and shook it. That was the pre-arranged signal that the air was sweet and he was feeling no ill effects; after which he untied the rope from round him. Then he felt a movement of the ladder that told him Blue had begun his descent. He flashed his torch upwards again and saw a blacker blob in the vapour cloud that quickly materialised into a human form. Then Blue was standing beside him. They flashed their torches in each other's faces and grinned, speech being quite useless in that hot space, vibrating to pounding and noise. Yet, if the terrific din had surprised Blue, his poker face concealed his surprise. Together they faced the big jet. Geoff flashed his torch left and right now and saw that the roof of the cavern was a dome that curved right to the floor. The floor itself dipped a little in the middle but, almost at their feet it was strewn with rock fragments. That would be the shattered rock lump that had fallen out of the roof.

They saw that they could walk down the centre of the floor dip and right under the jets. At a sign from Geoff they worked forward over the rock fragments. Then they both exclaimed together, though neither heard the other's voice. The smaller jet arched over and was splashing its water on the floor some ten yards ahead. Yet what surprised them was that the cavern stretched away ahead pretty much like a domed railway tunnel, but without its vertical walls. They paused a moment, then moving a little to the left to avoid the splash of the falling water from the small pressure head, they walked easily along beyond it. And, as far as their powerful torches would reach, the domed cave led on. And down the centre of the floor a little stream of clear water flashed back the white light of their torch beams.

It was this tunnel, then, twenty feet wide, that had carried away all the water that roared up out of the fissure behind them. Now, nearly all that water was hurtling up through the hole above to fall on to the surface rock of the ridge. The little stream at their feet, coming from the small jet, was all that was left of a stream twenty feet wide that must have carved out this tunnel.

Geoff groped and found a handkerchief and wiped his perspiring forehead. Then another thought struck him. He turned his face towards the opening, then back. Yes, there was no doubt of it—a slight coolness when he faced forward. Air was passing along the tunnel and out of the hole above. And, if it was passing out, it must be coming in. There must be another entrance to the cave!

Well, the others would be getting worried up above. He started to say as much to Blue, then realised they could talk only in dumb show. He turned and retraced his steps till he had climbed over the fallen rock once more and reached the ladder. Blue was close behind him but suddenly he stopped and flashed his torch on the fallen limestone. He beckoned and Geoff went back to him. Together they examined the rock fragment Blue had his hand on, then, still stooping, Geoff turned his head and grinned across at his friend. For, here was the answer to the thing that had puzzled him most of all—why a slab of immensely strong rock, five feet thick, should have collapsed from the drilling of a six-inch hole. It was plain to him now. A big piece of the slab was turned upside down. On one corner of it was the concave cut of the drill; and, on either side of the drill mark, the rock edge was discoloured. . . . It had already been cracked! The thrust of the water, the water's heat, contraction and expansion of the limestone from hot days and winter nights, all these together, as the rock 'roof' had gradually been worn thinner, had started that roughly circular crack in the roof's under side. Probably the fracture had penetrated somewhat higher just where they'd driven the short shaft and enabled Dogfoot to feel the vibration just there. They'd been drilling over a crack and hadn't known it, had been cursing the hardness of the rock! But the drill's assault had been all that great pounding jet had needed to complete that circular crack. And one other thing was plain. Like some of the age-old oasis flows of the Sahara, this pounding water would eventually, perhaps a century hence, have burst its own way out!

Monsieur used up a deal of French to welcome them out of the hole and shook each of them warmly by the hand. Then they all moved across to the truck at last to be away from the noise of the water and Geoff and Blue made their report.

"In short," Blue said at last, "it's a *nice* cave—and air-conditioned!"

"That's it," Geoff grinned. "Not one of those labyrinths of branching passages you can get lost in either—at least I'll be surprised if you could. I think we'll find it's just a tunnel. How far it goes is anybody's guess but there's no need to go down with a blessed string in your hand and things like that. A couple of lanterns to leave burning where branches fork off—if there *should* be any branches; torches, extra batteries for same, matches and a piece of chalk. The job's simple."

Barbara was laughing again now. Accustomed from childhood to the risks of work amongst horses and cattle, she was by no means easily frightened, and now, from what Geoff and Blue had said, she was satisfied exploring the cave would not prove the really dangerous task she had feared. It was agreed that she and Thornleigh and Monsieur should go home at once for the busy days had exhausted Thornleigh and the heat was trying for him. As for poor Monsieur, he was gasping steadily.

"Now mind no consorting with devils!" was all Barbara said as the car moved off, her laughing face tilted from the steering wheel as she leant to shift the gears. Eyes half closed to the glare, Geoff and Blue watched the car roll and twist its way towards the plain. When it swung away north-east a dozen steers, grazing near the track, threw up their heads and stared at it cheekily.

The two friends began checking their gear once more. Since his capture, Geoff had made a practice of wearing his automatic whenever he left the homestead. He began to take it off now, hesitated, then settled it back on his shoulder.

"It's warm enough down there without extras. Still a gun might come in handy to signal with if the cave's long enough to get us out of the racket of the water." He turned and looked at Dogfoot. From the beginning the black had shown no more liking than Monsieur for the vapour-filled blackness of the hole and they had already told him they wanted him to wait at the truck. The big fellow was quietly tending a small fire to make them tea before they left again. He said nothing but Geoff noticed his eyes were often on Blue and that they were full of uneasiness.

The quick meal over, Geoff glanced at his watch. "Ten past three. Okay, son, if you're ready, we'll hop down and see some more of the sights." He grinned at Dogfoot. Hang it, the old scout was worried stiff about Blue!

An unlighted lantern looped over his left arm, he climbed easily down the ladder into the thunderous noise and down to the floor. When Blue joined him, also carrying a lantern, he led the way along the tunnel to the point they had reached before. They did not pause but strode on abreast beside the little stream, for there was walking space of perhaps nine feet on either side of it. The walking was easy and the moist red sandstone a good gritty surface to their boots. But presently, when they had tramped perhaps a hundred yards, they saw what looked like the end of the tunnel. Then, their torch beams probing before them, they realised it was no dead end, but simply a left bend in the tunnel. It was by no means a sharp turn but rather like the easy bend of a small creek. Yet, as they tramped round it they were aware of a change. The noise of the water was no longer deafening.

"What do you think?" Geoff shouted, as they halted together. By way of answer, Blue held his torch steady till its long beam was killed by the darkness far ahead. The little glittering stream tapered off to a pin-point within the range of the white light. Geoff nodded and they moved on again. They tramped, saying nothing, for some three hundred yards. Then again their torch beams showed what looked like a wall ahead; and again it was a turn in the strange tunnel, this time to the right. Round it the noise of the water diminished so much that the cave seemed almost quiet. They had no longer need to shout. When he had got over the surprise of it, Geoff played his torch on the low roof.

"Take a look at that roof, feller. Darned near marble. It *is* marble."

Blue looked and nodded, then set his unlighted

hurricane lantern carefully on the hollowed floor, jerked out a handkerchief, and wiped his forehead.

"It just goes on!" He dug a box of matches from a pocket of his shorts, struck one and held it close to the floor. The flame burnt clearly and steadily, though its tip bent the least bit towards the way they had come.

"Good sign," Geoff commented. "The darned place is air-conditioned as you say! Well, if you've seen enough of this bit. . . ."

In five minutes' tramping they reached another bend—to the left; and presently another to the right. And here the noise was no more than a low murmuring. Again they stopped.

"Never knew a cave behave itself so well," Blue said. He looked at his watch. "Half past three."

"We've come half a mile, I'd say," Geoff answered. "Well, come on feller. But how about counting steps? That'll give us a rough idea where we're up to."

"That stream seems to have slowed down," the English lad commented as they tramped along again abreast. "What's the fall, do you reckon?"

Geoff dropped a match in the water and watched it. It floated along very slowly, seeming to stop altogether every six inches or so.

"Very slight, I'd say—ten feet in the mile, at most." Blue grunted his agreement.

"Glad to hear it. Don't want a lot of uphill work going back. Well, come on, fellow troglodyte! We might come to something, or then again we might surface in Africa."

From then on they walked in step and they stopped only three times in the next half hour—as they counted off a thousand steps.

"Three thousand," Blue said, then. "Don't want to hear your tally because I'm probably wrong but the main thing is it's time for a spell."

They sat down together on the damp sandstone floor.

"Three thousand," Blue said again, half an hour later.

"That makes three miles and a half!" Geoff answered. "And, according to my compass, very nearly straight west. Obviously we're deep enough down to be crossing under any valleys, for the ridge the bore is on doesn't run west that far. Well, I've heard of these caves running for miles but somehow I didn't expect this one to run far at all. It's half past four. Now what'll we do? It'll be dark up top at eight and they'll be getting het up again at the homestead if we're not back by then. If we go on for another half hour we can get back and out by seven—time to reach home by eight."

"Suits me," Blue answered. "But to-morrow we'll start early and fetch equipment for an African safari!" He looked over his shoulder, frowning.

"Now, that's funny!"

"What is, feller?"

"That echo! All the way here our voices have sounded hollow but they didn't what you'd call echo, exactly. But that time—yes, listen!"

"Yes, listen, listen, listen!" came faintly back to them from the darkness ahead!

They got to their feet at once and moved on to

the turn they could see ahead, expectancy in their faces; and, at once, they began to hear the footsteps, growing louder and louder as they tramped. They knew well they were all echoes but it was hard to dismiss the illusion that a dozen men were tramping with them, ahead, behind, on either side! They halted together and flashed their torches round and up. The domed walls had drawn apart, wide apart; the roof was now fully fifty feet overhead, the floor in front seemed to bend and plunge downwards into blackness, the little stream slipping down over it without a sound! As the white torch beams probed ahead and down and up, they realised they had tramped into a cave compared with which the one they had followed so far was somewhat like the long passage into an igloo!

Not quite that, however. Because, except for wide ledges running right and left around it, this cave was bottomless, it seemed—a chasm that plunged down and down into inky blackness. Both its sides were sheer cliffs. The end nearest them was a steep slope and the little stream simply shot down it. There was no sound of falling water. It slipped over the rock sill and down that unending slope into measureless darkness!

"Caesar!"

The word was a long-drawn exclamation—and it came back to them long-drawn, amplified, repeated in a dozen, a hundred, echoes that grew fainter one by one till the last was a long-drawn whisper! The two lads looked at each other in the light of their torches. When next Geoff spoke his voice was scarcely audible.

"Why, the place is a terrific size—a sort of underground gorge!"

Blue nodded without speaking. Finally he pointed to the left. "Looks safe enough round both sides of the chasm, though," he said quietly. "But how about if we go this way?"

The ledge to the left they found to be ten feet wide and rising gently ahead. They moved along it carefully. Three feet from the edge of the chasm they could stand up comfortably. To the left of that the ledge slipped in under an overhang of sandstone. They had gone fifty yards when Blue halted.

"Torch getting a bit played out. Got plenty batteries. Might as well change them, eh?"

Geoff agreed and they both sat down and slipped refills into the long barrels of their torches. That done, they kept moving, torch beams ever on the edge of the terrible chasm to their right. But gradually the clear walking space on the ledge widened to six feet though much of the ledge on their left was still overhung by the jutting sandstone. They tramped on abreast now for ten minutes. Several times Geoff moved close to the overhang, frowning in puzzlement. At last he stopped, his torch held steadily on the undercut sandstone, at the height of his head. Blue stopped too and, with their echoing footsteps stilled, the vast cavern was presently utterly silent. But Geoff felt something sharp under the sole of his right boot. Unconsciously he moved his foot and flicked it away. There came a faint tinkling, clear in that strange hollow quietness. He flashed his torch downwards. From the rock at his feet a small nickel buckle winked back the torch light! Blue saw him jerk forward to stare; then he, too, saw the buckle.

In that instant the hollow blackness was full of nightmare noise—peal after peal of devilish laughter flung back and forth in the vast cavern; fiendish, cackling echoes that grew louder as they multiplied! Peal after peal seemed to spring at the two boys across the great void! And, as if awaiting the dreadful chorus, the dark before them was suddenly pierced by lights—lights that flared and contracted, changed colour, yellow to green, and then red; that moved stealthily away and then stopped and loomed back towards them!

CHAPTER TWENTY-THREE

THE DOG PADS

PANIC SURGED in Geoff's brain. What but devils could laugh that horrible laughter, jumbling its terrible echoes in the blackness? Those lights that blazed and died and blazed again—they must be the eyes of devils! Then he had gripped Blue's arm and his torch beam held steady on two glaring eyes ten feet to the right of the others. As though his hand had told his thoughts, Blue flung his torch ray upon them too. . . . And right before the two boys, on the ledge across the chasm, a creature stood poised in the white beams—a great dog-like brute, its body full three feet long. A heavy mane doubled the thickness of its down-curved neck and its head was thrust out low towards them, the lips drawn back from long, white fangs. Its back and sides were spotted black and yellow, vivid in the torch beams. The hair under its neck seemed to writhe around its leering jaws. Suddenly the evil head tilted, the jaws jerked wide open and once again the mad laughter was flinging round their ears and the jeering echoes filled the vast cave from ink-black roof to the pitch dark of the chasm far below.

Blue felt Geoff's hand release his arm. There was a spurt of flame at his side, another and another and he could see the bullets spatter their hot lead on the rock beneath the great dog. The creature sprang up and backwards, twisting in the air, and seemed to fling itself in among the glaring eyes on the ledge. Then the eyes vanished all together and the torch beams showed a jumble of tawny bodies thrusting madly along the ledge.

When at last the echoes had died, Geoff thrust his automatic back in its holster and ran a hand with an upward sweep over his perspiring forehead.

"Phew! So that's what our devil is—a hyena! . . . a blessed African hyena! And . . . and, good lord, Blue, I should have known!"

"A hyena! . . . Heck, yes, that's what it was! A big ugly brute of a spotted hyena! And heck, feller, I'm not sure I wouldn't rather have a devil after all! The way the big brute threw back his head and laughed and laughed! But, in the name of the Prophet, how would an African hyena get here?"

"You tell *me*, son!" Geoff looked at his friend, facing him, feet apart. "The thing could have escaped from a circus menagerie, perhaps. Anyhow you saw the devilish brute yourself. Have you ever seen anything else like it? I stopped off on my way back from England and made a trip up to Nairobi in Tanganyika. I saw dozens of the savage brutes—heard 'em laugh, too—the same diabolical beast of a laugh we just heard, only in here it was amplified and collected ten thousand beastly echoes. But I should have known when I heard it in the open that evening with you and Barbara! I *did* think of it but the idea seemed idiotic—fantastic! But caves! They told me in Nairobi that any cave was sure to be full of the brutes. All I wish is I'd seen this one before I heard him laugh. Gosh, feller, was I scared!"

"Hmph! And the others were dingoes! Well, from what I've heard of spotted hyenas, they're natural-born killers and pack hunters too. They should chum up with dingoes pretty well. Hang it their eyes match anyhow. They looked lovely glaring red and yellow and green from across that darned awful chasm. But why didn't you shoot to kill, feller?"

"Hanged if I know, Blue. Can't say I like killing things much. They're noxious animals, I know, but I don't suppose that joker does any real harm, away out here."

"Well, they seem to have scooted out the way we're headed," Blue said. "Only they're on the opposite side of this outsize hole or whatever it is."

"I'm game to bet they bolted into the open ahead, there, where the chasm probably finishes. But—why, good gosh, man—that buckle we found!"

He wheeled and flashed his torch on the rock floor and Blue stooped to help with the search.

Within five seconds they had found it again. Geoff picked it up. It lay in his left palm and twinkled in the torch beams.

A saddle-bag buckle, right enough," Blue said quietly. "Heavily nickelled. Could be a year old or twenty. So what?"

Geoff shook his head.

"I thought at first it might mean somebody was hiding up here. But those dogs could have brought it in—at any rate that darned hyena could. I believe the beggars have a mania for chewing up anything made of leather."

"Well, we haven't got to stick around guessing, feller. We seem to be finding things, this last ten minutes. How about pushing on?"

Geoff hesitated, then nodded.

"Okay Blue. I was going to take a good look at this shelving sandstone that arches out over the ledge. But that can wait. Lead on, feller."

They moved on again slowly, searching the ledge surface, now, as they walked. The ledge seemed to be twisting a little to the left. They travelled perhaps a hundred yards, keeping always a close watch on the lip of rock on their right that formed the brink of the terrible chasm. Blue, still leading the way, was moving more quickly now. Then, suddenly, he stopped.

Geoff ranged up beside him his torch trained on the spot ahead upon which Blue had focused his, on a blackish, circular patch on the red sandstone floor. Saying nothing, they moved forward slowly again; but within ten strides each boy's surmise was confirmed. They were looking at a patch of rock burnt black by a camp fire.

"Good gosh!" Geoff exclaimed softly and slowly. "So it *has* been a hide-out! We'll be. . . ."

But he had flashed his torch sideways and what he saw this time cut short his speech. It was a hammer-headed miner's pick lying flat on the sandstone!

Without speaking, Geoff stepped across and picked it up, holding it by the rusty head. His torch beam showed up the rust of the metal, red on one side, but turned almost black on the side that had rested on the rock floor. He moved his hand along the handle. Next instant he was staring at the handle as at a ghost. He stared while one could count ten. When he turned to Blue his voice was a whisper.

"Blue! . . . Uncle George . . . This pick belonged to Uncle George! . . . Look!"

Blue was beside him in a stride and peered at a mark on the handle, the tip of Geoff's finger touching it. GHW, in well-formed letters, neatly burnt into the wood.

"George Henry Warburton!" Geoff was saying. "He . . . it's burnt on with the little branding iron Uncle used. Every wooden handled tool he had on the farm was branded with it. Why. . . ."

Blue Campbell was not easily surprised but his friend's next move astonished him. Geoff had dropped the pick and was pointing at the underside of the sandstone overhang that formed a sort of false roof over the wide ledge.

"Blue!" Once more his voice was a whisper. "There under the gritstone overhang! Opal dirt! Opal dirt up under the sandstone! And it's chockful of colour potch!"

For men with a fortune within their grasp time does not exist. The boys' watches ticked on and on while a little pile of black stones grew slowly; black stones banded with bright red bands. They were piled on Geoff's shirt spread on the rock. Geoff knelt beside it, his bare back to the chasm behind him and the lantern light gleaming on his sweat-damp face. He had laid his automatic, holster and all, on the rock floor near the fire-blackened circle twenty feet away. As he knelt now, his knife blade flashed in the yellow light, cleaning each new stone the thudding pick dislodged with the mullock. Blue, sweating freely, was taking his turn with the pick, swinging it with quick, short strokes up under the sloping rock roof as Geoff had shown him how. The mullock they had scraped carefully aside into a bank eight feet long and two high, at right angles to the ledge. On the end closest to Blue they had set one lantern. The other lantern, burning brightly, stood on the floor close to the lip of the wide ledge, so that it lighted the edge of the terrible chasm. And, time completely forgotten, they worked on, knife and pick flashing in the yellow beams.

They could not see the red sun flinging level rays across the ridges above them, nor the two horsemen who rode slowly over a ridge top.

One of the riders reined up suddenly, pointing eastward.

"What the devil's that, Graster? It looks like water flashing in the sun!"

The other glanced aside, drew rein and followed Maddon's pointing arm. Away to the east something flashed on a ridge top; and, as his tired pacer steadied and stood still, the flashing changed to a steady beam of white, like the beam from a mirror flung in their faces. But Graster cursed.

"Only a patch of this confounded marbly limestone catching the sun, you fool. There's no water up this end of Thornleigh's run. I only wish there was!"

Maddon turned a surly face to his companion.

"Better be careful who you're calling a fool, Graster. As to that, you nearly led us into a police trap up north—as near as hang it!"

It was plain the speech angered Graster and he looked at the other with narrowed eyes; but, before he spoke his right hand slid forward to the stock of his rifle.

"All right. And now we're travelling south. But if you don't want to stay with me, cut loose, you fool." He watched Maddon closely for five seconds. When no reply came his lip curled in a sneer. Then he leant forward to shorten the bridle reins that had slipped a little through his left hand, and touched his heels to his mount. The movement focused his eyes on the rock surface ahead and, even as the black pacer moved, he reined her in again. Maddon looked at him angrily as he stared downwards. But this time Graster was pointing.

"Maddon! Look! Those lines on the rock, there, all meeting! . . . They're tracks . . . pads! Pads made by dogs; and they lead up to that hole there!"

He turned to the man beside him, the sinking sun full on his excited face. "Dog pads, worn in the limestone! leading to a hole in the rock! Man they're what Warburton gabbled about when he was delirious in Hamery's pub!"

CHAPTER TWENTY-FOUR

THE LAST LAUGH

GEOFF NEVER knew what made him look round; but, with his one swift glance, his right hand flashed out and sent the nearer lantern crashing. In the same second that he flung sideways, Maddon's gun filled the vast cave with thunderous echoes. The bullet struck beside Geoff as he rolled, another slashed through his left arm. He felt the mullock beneath him as a third bullet splashed the rock floor he had left. Then his shoulder scraped the rock overhang and he was over the heap. But a jeering voice was speaking.

"That's the way I like to see you move young Mason. You had fun with Maddon at the gorge, didn't you? And you and your friends had a lot of fun later. Been laughing ever since, haven't you? But it's the last laugh that counts, Mason. You've come to the end of your trail, you and your red-headed friend, squirming under the rock there! But you've lived long enough to give us all we want. We've got you and we've got the opals. You've even gouged some for us, I see! And you've even put a spare gun here handy for us! Most obliging! Here you are, Dirk. Now you can have one in each hand!"

Geoff's mind raced as he listened. Maddon, he knew, had only to move ten feet to his left to get past the mullock heap and shoot him to pieces.

But Blue . . . Blue was back under the shelf there, looking into the gun muzzles . . . two automatics in Maddon's hands and Graster's rifle. The killers stood close together, waiting to kill. Blue might throw the pick and try to scramble from under the rock, but these devils would shoot him down before he ever got to his feet. Geoff's torch had been behind him and there'd been no time to snatch it; worse, his knife had gone scuttering along the floor when he crashed the lantern. . . . The mullock. There wasn't a stone in it big enough to hurt a man; not a pebble, even. He would just have to scratch up a handful of the biggest of the gravel and fling it as he sprang to try and spoil Maddon's aim. It was suicide, yet, to wait was certain death for them both. He could feel hot blood pouring down his left arm as he thrust his right along the rock floor back behind him, where some bigger grit might have spilled down from the mullock. His fingers searched desperately. . . .

But, instead of grit, they found something else; a smooth, curved surface of polished wood!

In that moment, with his life measured in seconds, he saw his uncle's eager eyes in the glare of the burning house. A dead man's voice seemed to whisper in his ear. . . . A dead man had thrust a rifle into his hand!

His thoughts and his groping had needed no more than seconds. As his hands moved swiftly behind the mound Graster's jeering voice was still in his ears.

"Pity you didn't manage to crash the other light over, Mason!"

With the last word, Geoff flung up on his knees and, as though all part of the lightning movement, the heavy Winchester he held belched red fire. As its roar filled the great cavern, both Maddon's hands jerked up together, a queer, convulsive jerk that flung his guns spinning into the void behind him, as though they were part of a juggler's trick. But the same convulsion seemed to fling his body at Graster, his hands before him, their great fingers opening and closing. With a sharp oath Graster drew up his right foot and lashed out savagely. The kick saved him by a hair's breadth from the death grip of the clutching fingers; but his rifle was snatched from his hands and gone. It glinted once in the lamplight, then it was gone with the dead man, plummeting into the blackness.

With the echoes' thunder all round him, Geoff was dragging at a jammed loading bolt. Seeing he could not free it, he sprang up, only to crash his head against the rock above. In the split second as he sprawled forward he saw Graster spring away and Blue scrambling out towards him. Then he knew no more.

He recovered consciousness lying on the smooth rock of the ridge side, his head pillowed on Blue's knee. The daylight was gone and a first-quarter moon hung in the western sky. His left arm was bandaged tightly and Blue was bathing his forehead. He frowned up into his friend's face.

"Ha! Here we are again!" Blue said. "But it's no use scowling at me like that, feller. I didn't hit you."

Geoff sat up and summoned a grin.

"Cæsar, I'm as weak as a cat! What goes on, son?"

His friend told him a brief story. He had got the bleeding of Geoff's arm stopped, then dragged him out of the cave the way Graster had gone, by way of the dingoes' get-out. By that time it was dark and he had signalled Dogfoot with a kerosene flare made from his shirt. Dogfoot had arrived on the run and Blue had sent him to catch Maddon's horse which the hunter had seen making towards the bore, apparently having seen or smelt the water.

"And now he's on his way to the homestead," Blue said. "I wouldn't have sent him but we've given them enough darned worry already."

Suddenly he frowned, looking eastward.

"But I guess I started him too late, after all. There's carlights out on the plain now." He turned again to Geoff. "How goes it? No doubt about it you specialise in bumps on the head. You've got a lump on top this time that'd do for a cricket ball! But it was the blood you lost that kept you out for so long, I reckon. By the way, here's the opals, tied up in your shirt."

Geoff took the heavy bundle, but set it beside him without untying it.

"There's more yet, Blue. And they're ours. That's the way Uncle George wanted it. But . . . Uncle George's rifle. . . ."

For answer Blue stooped and picked up a Winchester thirty-two from the rock. Its barrel was rusted, red on one side, black on the other like the pick-head. Its breach was actually crusted with rust and the slide fouled with fine grit. The bolt was half open now, a bullet jammed in the slide, its lead nose pointing outwards. Geoff laid the heavy gun across his knees.

"The bullet in the barrel. . . ." He stopped. Blue nodded, then spoke quietly.

"That bullet waited there four years . . . and got the man it waited for." He paused. "A close call, feller! And darned good shooting!"

They speculated as to how the Winchester had come to be so far along under the overhang of sandstone; so far that they had not seen it.

"Uncle George would have slept in the cave beside that fire and he'd lay the rifle and saddle bags around handy I reckon. But we know he was half-dazed with malaria. That ungodly laugh must have broken his nerve and he just grabbed his saddle and made a break."

"That's about it," Blue agreed. "And the dogs attended to his saddle bags, or that darned hyena did. And they dragged the rifle up under that shelf where you put your hand on it. Might have mistaken it for a bone."

Presently they could see long light beams swinging to and fro across the ridges as the approaching car wound its way towards them. Blue lit the flare again while Geoff, with the last of his friend's unfortunate shirt saturated in kerosene released and cleaned the breach of the rifle and refilled the magazine.

Thornleigh and Monsieur were in the car and Thornleigh had brought three native stockmen and Dogfoot as far as the truck. He had brought, also, an ample supply of provisions together with the first aid materials that outback dwellers take along as a matter of course, and some clothes from the tent. The bullet had passed right through Geoff's arm. Within twenty minutes Monsieur, at Blue's request, had renewed the dressing and put the arm in a sling and all were drinking tea.

"Well, thank God for that," Thornleigh said simply, when he had heard their story. "And so you've made your opal find after all, boys!"

Monsieur looked over the opals for them, snipping carefully at some with a pair of snips Thornleigh found for him among the fencing tools in the tool box of the car. Geoff was amazed at the precision with which the old Frenchman handled the clumsy snips. But when Monsieur spoke at last he was non-committal.

"I think there is some good stone, Messieurs, but there is only one way to value the opal after all. 'E must be cut and polish with good tool. Ze better ze stone ze more dangerous to fool with 'im. You must be patient, Messieurs."

But Blue and Geoff thanked him warmly, knowing well they were being given the advice of an expert.

"Well, now, how about taking a look at the cave?" Blue invited.

"*Non*, another time," Monsieur demurred hastily. "I stay with M'sieur Geoff!"

But, torch in hand and moving cautiously because of his strained back muscles, Thornleigh crawled after Blue through the crevice that led into the cavern. While they were away Monsieur plied Geoff with more tea and many questions concerning the hyena. Some ten minutes later Blue and Thornleigh returned. The latter shook his head as he leant on a mudguard of his car.

"Amazing place! And, apparently, just that one freak pocket of opal dirt, nearly all of it well-coloured potch. No indications anywhere else under all that queer gritstone. Makes you wonder if a good many fortunes weren't washed away down into that chasm. . . . And M'sieur's devil is a hyena taken to the bush! We saw no sign of the dog pack, though. As you say, they must have bolted round the end of the chasm when Geoff fired those shots and taken to the ridges. Well, now, how long will it take to gouge the rest of your opal dirt?"

"Blue and Dogfoot should have it all down to-morrow morning," Geoff grinned. "But now you've brought us all the home comforts, Mr. Thornleigh, we'll all stand by here to-night, just in case."

The cattle-man nodded.

"As you wish, Geoff. But as for Graster, it looks as though he'll try and cross to the west and then work south from soak to soak. It's a long chance. But you should be in bed with that arm. How about him, Henri?"

"'E *should* be in bed, yes. But if 'e will not go . . ." Monsieur shrugged.

"Then, in that case we'll get back. Barbara . . ." the cattle-man paused and his eyes twinkled as he corrected himself. "They're all pretty anxious at home."

"With you I will make ze journey to Burramoola

when you 'ave all ze opal, M'sieur Blue," Monsieur offered. "There is things to do about sending ze jewel by post an' air mail which I am well used to see to. Again I say, to make ze value 'ere I will not risk. With ze opal one stone 'e is worth much, ze nex' perhaps, what you say, five bob! There is undoubtedly some good opal 'ere, yet all must be cut, Messieurs, and Jacques will attend quickly."

The old man got into the car with Thornleigh. Blue went with them to the bore to bring the truck across to where they intended to spend the night. When the car had driven away Geoff lay and watched its headlamps stabbing to and fro and listened to its engine growing fainter. Then he rolled over to ease his arm and looked out over the tumble of red limestone, ridge beyond twisted ridge, grotesque and silent in the moonlight. . . . Thornleigh had said nothing at all about the loss of his beautiful mare. That swine would probably kill her in the desert.

Far to the westward the moonlight winked on a foam-flecked bridle bit as Graster spurred the jaded pacer. Mile after mile she held the pace, but with each mile her weariness made it harder for her to keep her feet on the rock surface. At last, near a ridge top, she stumbled badly but her rally to his spurring reassured Graster. She'd get him away yet! She had the blood! It was not courage she lacked, however, but safe footing for the thrust of her flying hoofs.

Her tumbling fall on the crest of the ridge surprised him completely.

Even so, he might have got clear if the stirrup had

not clutched his boot. A powerful lunge and she had found her feet once more but that lunge snapped the sun-perished throat strap of her bridle. The bridle pulled off and her head was free. . . . But only her head was free. A heavy form hung from one stirrup, dragging her sideways, a grotesque form, its arms and legs flung wide. One look and she gathered her haunches and sprang away, lashing madly at the thing that seemed to clutch and menace her, her hoofs thudding and thudding upon it, slashing and battering till it dragged, a lifeless lump, down the slope and up the next, staining the reddish rock face with a darker red; and then, at last, the slow-tearing leather broke. The stirrup jerked from it, clinked down on the rock and lay still beside the man it had killed.

The mare's terror had sent her back on her tracks. It passed at last and she slowed and slowed till she was plodding steadily eastward. Flanks heaving still, she halted once as though to check her direction, then plodded on again, back to the saltbush plain she knew and the strange water she had seen and smelt in the sunset. The moon set while she plodded and the sky filled with stars; and once she saw dim forms on a ridge crest . . . and eyes that glared green.

She had travelled a mile more, the saddle creaking in time with her light tread. The small sounds of her breathing were all in that wide silence. She had forgotten the green-eyed dingo pack that had spread out to pass her. She knew nothing of the macabre feasting already begun on that ridge top to the westward. But suddenly she halted with a quick rasp of hoofs on the rock, her head flung high and her nostrils flaring wide.

For, across the desolation behind her, came terrible laughter, peal after peal, insane and devilish, flinging past and around her and far up among the stars!

CHAPTER TWENTY-FIVE

Au Revoir

THE TWO troopers from Burramoola left the summer-house, filled now with laughing guests and walked across to the tent for a yarn with Geoff and Blue. Micky the Tinker, yarding the stock horses, had found the black pacer among them, carrying a saddle minus one stirrup. The troopers had borrowed Matoorlie horses and ridden into the ridges. On the second day they had scared up a little flock of crows . . . and found the missing stirrup.

"Well, I must say you make things interesting on Matoorlie," the younger of the men said this morning as he accepted an invitation to sit on Blue's bunk. "That bore is one of the biggest surprises I've come across." He turned to his companion. "I was thinking about that hyena these chaps saw, Bob."

"We also heard him," Blue said grimly.

"*And* heard," the cheerful trooper resumed. "Do you remember that business of a car trailer that broke loose and rolled down a bank near Turramuk about four years ago? How far would Turramuk be east of here—about four hundred miles?"

Calwell nodded. "About that. Have to get you transferred to the detective branch, Doug," he said quietly. "But you could be right at that. There were two cages on that trailer. One of them busted open. It contained two spotted hyenas and one of the brutes was killed. The other was never seen again. He got away all right and he could have hunted his way four hundred miles out here easily enough. Looks as though he found a nice cave when he got here and decided to stay and hunt with the dingo pack."

Calwell had a long quiet talk with Lakker which seemed to make the little man very happy indeed, and both troopers left next day. But, for the remainder of the week, car after car drove up to the Matoorlie homestead and on out to the bore. Everybody called it "the bore," though they gazed in amazement at the great pressure head hissing up out of the gaping hole a five-foot-deep drill shaft had broken out. Geoff and Blue and Madame and Monsieur helped to do the honours. Guests stayed overnight and some stayed several nights. Indeed every shed of the homestead seemed to be sheltering a car or cars of some sort and one or two that defied description. On four evenings hilarious parties swam and splashed in the hot water of the rock lagoon. Most of the visitors took snaps of the bore and the Matoorlie people.

"Some of those snaps will be in the Brisbane papers," Thornleigh chuckled. "We'll have quite a few opal gougers out here, too, to explore your cave boys. I'm afraid they'll find no opals but if you told them that they'd be even more anxious to come. However, some of them might stay and work for me. I'll be wanting more stockmen pretty soon now."

The day the last car drove away the homestead

seemed almost deserted. In the afternoon Geoff and Blue relaxed with Monsieur in the summer-house and Thornleigh was up at the south end of the run to see about the building of branding yards there, for the south end, hitherto so little used, was veritably a new run.

It was cool in the summer-house and Geoff lay back and grinned at an argument going on between Lakker and the joey, who now appeared to have settled for life in the Matoorlie garden.

"Me an' me boys 'as got something better to do than plant seedlin' lettuces for a contraption like you!" Lakker was saying. "I don't mind you havin' a couple, mind y', but not a couple o' dozen! You stick to milk, mostly, do you hear?"

The speaker shook his rake at his hearer and limped past the summer-house door along the path. Monsieur looked after him thoughtfully.

"Ze scoundrel Maddon, M'sieur Geoff . . . You shoot 'im in ze leg, yes?"

There was a little silence.

"I couldn't risk it, M'sieur," Geoff said quietly. "I shot him dead."

Again there was silence. Then Monsieur sighed.

"Ah well," he answered. "It was perhaps as well. Otherwise, assuredly 'e would be 'ang by ze neck. Me I do not like that way, even for ze Boche!"

The telephone shrilled in the quiet house and they heard Barbara's quick step and her voice.

"Oh, very well, Margaret . . . just a moment please." Then she called softly from the house. "For you, M'sieur. Brisbane calling."

"Ah, that will be Jacques," M'sieur said and got

up and rolled indoors, as though phone calls across Queensland were nothing to hurry about. But Geoff and Blue exchanged glances. If this was Jacques then they would know in a matter of minutes now, what their opals were worth!

They could hear Monsieur speaking French in short vigorous phrases and then there were silences when apparently he listened to long explanations. Finally he made a long speech himself that suggested he was very perturbed indeed. Finally, at long last, the receiver clicked back on the hook.

The old Frenchman came out to them slowly. He held a sheet of paper in his hand. He sat down slowly and heavily, his eyes on the paper and his face full of sadness. Then he looked up.

"It is of ze opal I speak, Messieurs," he said sadly. "And I 'ave much to say. For many young men, Messieurs, it is better to 'ave not much money. For them money is ze damnation! As ze young men with not much I 'ave love you both." He paused and his kindly face seemed sadder still. "Once, M'sieur Geoff, I am offer you ze job. Always I offer it. Also I 'ave one for M'sieur Blue. And not only now I offer it, but always. I tell you, Messieurs, every man must 'ave ze work. Ze young man with much money 'e is not always 'appy. If 'e 'ave no job 'e is, what you say, ze playboy, an' then 'e is ze abomination and make much trouble. I pray you, Messieurs, remember this—for now you are ze well-to-do young men. I congratulate you!"

For a moment the summer-house was silent. Then Geoff had sprung, laughing, to his feet and Blue with him.

"By heavens, M'sieur, if you didn't lead me up the garden! I thought you were letting us down to bad news—to saying the opals were no good!"

Monsieur looked up at them, his face filled with astonishment.

"Ze opal—without value! *Non*, *non*! Jacques 'e is astonish. Here is ze figure, Messieurs. See, two stone 'e is not much but ze rest 'e is ze best flame stone an' ze best harlequin pattern, Messieurs! Look you at ze figure."

Geoff and Blue looked down eagerly at the sheet. At the bottom of rows of figures which Monsieur must have been taking down during the long silences over the phone, they read the total valuation —£43,784. They looked up and exchanged incredulous grins. Then Geoff, still grinning, whirled and called through the doorway.

"Barbara!"

"You see there is six stone ver' beautiful," Monsieur continued casually. "Jacques value 'im ver' high. If you wish, after you 'ave ze check valuation, we will buy ze parcel entire. If you prefer not, Jacques will arrange ze market. . . . *Mon Dieu*!"

Apparently gems worth thousands were no novelty to Monsieur; but finding two young men and a girl suddenly holding hands and romping round and round his chair surprised him considerably. He said as much, smiling up at Blue.

"Believe me, M'sieur," Blue assured him, "though well known as a steady character, I'd dance a hula-hula with a grizzly bear for fourteen thousand pounds! Anyhow, you looked so down in the dumps, M'sieur, and you sounded broken-hearted. I thought we'd missed out badly!"

And immediately Monsieur was sad again.

"Ah, it is for poor Madeleine of ze good Jacques that I am grieve, Messieurs! Ze so small Madeleine. 'E 'ave ze measle!"

Whether or not they would have been able to share Monsieur's desolation, their shouts of laughter had already brought Madame and Mrs. Thornleigh from the house and poor Madeleine's measles were temporarily forgotten in the congratulations that followed. In fact the rejoicings lasted till Dick Thornleigh returned and then began again. Finally after toasts had been drunk, Geoff and Blue went in search of Dogfoot.

"The feller's already in Thornleigh's pay for finding that water," Geoff said. "It took Thornleigh half a day to make him understand he had a right to a divvy. You'll have to explain this show to him."

"We'll just have to invest his share for him in gilt edged," Blue answered. "It should hand him £10 a week in interest after it's taxed."

They sat down on either side of Dogfoot, and Blue, with the aid of ten one pound notes, set to work to explain to the big hunter that his share of the opal find was £10 a week for life. But the discussion kept them both gesticulating till tea-time for Dogfoot wanted his wealth expressed in terms of alarm clocks, tobacco, so many shirts per year, so many pairs of trousers etc. The tent became littered with little piles of shorts, packets of tobacco, cakes of soap and everything else procurable in any quantity. Dogfoot surveyed them all at last and for the first time Geoff saw him excited. Then the giant hunter terminated the session with a long, excited speech in pidgin that was too much even for Blue. As for Geoff he had to cover his laughter by springing up and thumping the speaker on the back.

After tea Blue and Thornleigh pleaded sheer laziness and asked to be excused when Mrs. Thornleigh suggested a drive in the cool. The others went in Monsieur's Packard, Barbara driving, for Geoff's arm was far from healed. When they returned an hour later she and Geoff put away the car.

"Geoff *Mason*!" she laughed as they stood, presently, beside one closed door. "How could any girl possibly be as nice as that? Anyway you haven't known me a month, yet, and most of the time you've been miles away across the run or else down in that awful cave! Still . . . you *are* the nicest boy!"

The only other occupant of the shed was the dingo cub, tied up in there each night. Barbara's speech just didn't make sense to him at all. He puzzled about it, his forehead creased in a deep frown. Then he gave it up, dropped his head on his paws and went to sleep.

Next morning after breakfast Geoff found Monsieur smoking in the garden and broached a subject that had been in his mind for a considerable time. But when he had finished speaking the old Frenchman's kindly face was beaming.

"Of course I am not offend, *mon ami*! I would be, what you say, ver' childish. *Au contraire*, I am please, an' Madame also, that you think of your friend so!"

The result of that conspiracy was that the Minton acquired yet another owner—Blue.

"You fell for her the day you saw her, feller," Geoff laughed when he and Blue had finally talked the matter out. "And a car like that has a right to a top-line driver, anyhow, which I'm not."

The next two weeks brought news of the sale of a West Queensland motor transport business. Blue secured an option on it and set to work immediately teaching Dogfoot to drive a truck. He hoped, he said, to persuade his father to give up the show business and manage the office side of the business. Geoff wanted to interview boring plant suppliers in Brisbane. But it was time for Madame and Monsieur to return home and, with unlimited stock water on Matoorlie, Thornleigh meant to go east and buy cattle as soon as he could.

"That leaves you and Barbara with nothing to do, Mother," the cattle-man chuckled. "Unless, of course, you come to Brisbane for a holiday. We can all leave as soon as Jim Fawkner and Bill get back. Jim writes to say he'll be home on Friday. Can you be ready to start on Monday? I think Henri and Marie would like to go then or next day."

The foreman and Bill arrived in the midst of a swishing desert storm but they couldn't wait to see the new water and the others drove with them to the south end of the big run. They exchanged amused glances as the stockmen stared, incredulous. At last the foreman turned to them.

"Somebody kick me hard," he pleaded. "They told me in Burramoola you 'ad a gusher, Dick, but I couldn't have believed 'em because I can't believe what I'm seein' now—gushin' water an' a lagoon with waves on it where there should be 'ot rock! An', heck, if them steers ain't havin' a drink of it!"

"Take a good look at them, Jim," Thornleigh chuckled. "Full and cheeky, desert wind and all! Three weeks ago I'd have taken a pound a head for them!"

Monday came and the three cars left the homestead together, Blue and Dogfoot and the dingo pup in the Minton. But Dogfoot consented to leave the joey in Ben Lakker's care. The arrangement appeared to suit the joey very well for, having had his hand shaken and his ears pulled by all the travellers, he watched cheerfully while they drove away, then hopped into a shade the better to admire Ben, waving his rake from the gate, along with his staff of three black-fellows waving hoes.

By the end of the first day, Dogfoot was driving the big Minton sports with ease and precision.

"Keeps the beggar interested," Blue growled. "Too many early emu chickens about on the plains —a blessed dozen to a family! I've got to keep his mind off *them*!"

Next morning the Packard removed the north-east corner of Takatoo's General Store and that night she jolted the Durracot Post Office off its piles. Having, as usual, settled for the damage, Monsieur examined a small dent in her off-side mudgard, and shook his head.

"It may be that 'e is used to ze brick wall," he said sadly to Geoff and Blue. "But there is yet twelve 'undred kilometre! M'sieur Geoff, do you and Barbara drive 'im, or again perhaps we are all in ze 'ole, *mais oui*!"

THE END

GLOSSARY

Agistment: The price paid for cattle pasturing on land.

Bowser: A kerbside petrol pump.

Duco: The enamel paint on a motor car.

Gazooker: A slang word meaning "fat-head."

Glove box: The pocket in the dashboard of a car.

Joey: A young animal, especially a kangaroo or wallaby.

Kaikai: Food.

Lubra: A black woman.

Mullock: Rubbish, especially mining refuse.

Myall: A wild Australian black.

Pisé: Rammed earth used for making walls and floors.

Potch: A blackish crust of rock encasing the real opals. There may be a mass of potch with a number of opals embedded in it. Again, potch may contain red and green streaks but no opals at all.

Saltbush: Any Australian shrubby plant of the goose-foot family.

Skillion room: A room roofed by a projecting or veranda roof, jutting out from the main building.

Spinifex: A coarse, hard, tussocky grass that covers vast areas in Australia.

Spruiker: A side-show owner who shouts an account of what he has to offer.

Tanna bush: An Australian shrub of the acacia family.

Wilga trees: Small drought-resisting trees, the twigs and leaves of which are excellent stock fodder. The trees are especially valuable because they can withstand a certain amount of "lopping," so that branches can be cut off and fed to sheep and cattle in time of drought.

Wommera: A three-foot stick that may be said to double the length of a spear-thrower's arm. One end of it notches into the tailing end of the spear for throwing. The wommera, of course, is retained in the hand after each throw.